"Is It Over? Are You Married?" Tuck, His Nephew, Demanded Of Jed.

"Yes he is," Judge Morgan replied.

Tuck breathed a sigh of relief, then looked at his uncle. "You're not very good at this, are you?"

Jed barely glanced at him. His gaze was still on Brenna. They had stepped apart, but their fingers were still entwined. He wanted to hang on forever.

The temptation was incredible. He knew he didn't dare. Carefully he loosened his fingers and eased them out of her grasp. Hers fell to her side.

In the babble and jostle of the room where they had been joined, now they stood alone.

She was his wife.

His *wife*.

Dear Reader,

The holidays are always a busy time of year, and this year is no exception! Our "banquet table" is chock-full of delectable stories by some of your favorite authors.

November is a time to come home again—and come back to the miniseries you love. Dixie Browning continues her TALL, DARK AND HANDSOME series with *Stryker's Wife*, which is Dixie's 60th book! This MAN OF THE MONTH is a reluctant bachelor you won't be able to resist! Fall in love with a footloose cowboy in *Cowboy Pride*, book five of Anne McAllister's CODE OF THE WEST series. Be enthralled by *Abbie and the Cowboy*—the conclusion to the THREE WEDDINGS AND A GIFT miniseries by Cathie Linz.

And what would the season be without HOLIDAY HONEYMOONS? You won't want to miss the second book in this cross-line continuity series by reader favorites Merline Lovelace and Carole Buck. This month, it's a delightful wedding mix-up with *Wrong Bride, Right Groom* by Merline Lovelace.

And that's not all! *In Roared Flint* is a secret baby tale by RITA Award winner Jan Hudson. And Pamela Ingrahm has created an adorable opposites-attract story in *The Bride Wore Tie-Dye*.

So, grab a book and give *yourself* a treat in the middle of all the holiday rushing. You'll be glad you did.

Happy reading!

Lucia Macro

Senior Editor
and the editors of Silhouette Desire

Please address questions and book requests to:
Silhouette Reader Service
U.S.: 3010 Walden Ave., P.O. Box 1325, Buffalo, NY 14269
Canadian: P.O. Box 609, Fort Erie, Ont. L2A 5X3

ANNE McALLISTER
COWBOY PRIDE

SILHOUETTE *Desire*®

Published by Silhouette Books

America's Publisher of Contemporary Romance

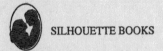

SILHOUETTE BOOKS

ISBN 0-373-76034-5

COWBOY PRIDE

Books by Anne McAllister

Silhouette Desire

*Cowboys Don't Cry #907
*Cowboys Don't Quit #944
*Cowboys Don't Stay #969
*The Cowboy and the Kid #1009
*Cowboy Pride #1034

*Code of the West

ANNE McALLISTER

was born and raised in California, land of surfers, swimmers and beach-volleyball players. She spent her teenage years researching them in hopes of finding the perfect hero. It turned out, however, that a few summer weeks spent at her grandparents' in Colorado and all those hours in junior high spent watching Robert Fuller playing Jess Harper on "Laramie" were formative. She was fixated on dark, handsome, intense, lone-wolf types. Twenty-nine years ago she found the perfect one prowling the stacks of the university library and married him. They now have four children, three dogs, a fat cat and live in the Midwest (as in "Is this heaven?" "No, it's Iowa.") in a reasonable facsimile of semiperfect wedded bliss to which she always returns—even though the last time she was in California, she had lunch with Robert Fuller.

For my father,
Seth P. Jenkins, Sr.
1914-1995

There are all kinds of legacies,
but the best one is love.

One

"I'm going to take art lessons," Tuck said.

Jed McCall turned from the stove to stare at his nephew, as amazed as if Tuck had just announced he was going to run away and join the circus. As far as Jed was concerned, a circus would have made more sense. *"Art lessons?"*

Tuck nodded. "Felicity thinks it would be a good idea." He lifted his version of the don't-mess-with-me McCall chin and met Jed's gaze, unblinking. He didn't have to look up as far this year, Jed noticed. The boy was ten now and getting kind of lanky—not quite to the awkward stage yet, but close. Like a pup trying to grow into its feet. Jed remembered the feeling.

"Felicity thinks that, does she?" He banged the frying pan on top of the stove and slapped in a knife's worth of congealed bacon grease. It sizzled and spattered. He cracked an egg and wished for an instant it was Felicity Jones's meddling head.

His boss Taggart Jones's new wife, Felicity, had been Tuck's teacher last year. Obviously, even though Felicity had passed the boy on, she was still keeping her hand in—and her suggestions. In fact, Jed liked Felicity—when she wasn't meddling in his life. A pretty blonde with dimples to die for, Felicity had a smile that would curl a man's toes and a heart as big as the Montana sky.

She'd come to Elmer only the year before, but it hadn't taken her long to make an impact on the community. Especially on Taggart.

Jed had been as surprised as anyone when they'd got married last November. Still, he thought Taggart had made a good choice this time. After his disastrous first marriage, Taggart hadn't wanted a woman in his life any more than Jed did, though for very different reasons—and he probably wouldn't have one, either, Jed thought, if it hadn't been for his meddling daughter, Becky.

What was it with women? he wondered now, grimacing. He cracked another egg next to the first and slopped some of the melting grease over both.

"Well, good for Felicity," he said after a moment's reflection. "An' she's probably right, too," he added honestly. "You do have talent. But where the hell does she think you're going to get art lessons around here?"

Elmer, Montana, seven miles away, was the closest town. And while Elmer was useful for getting your horse trailer welded or buying milk and bread, it wasn't exactly the hub of the Western cultural world. Among its 218 or so inhabitants, art teachers were not exactly thick on the ground.

Now if Felicity had suggested acting lessons . . .

Thanks to the sudden influx of rich California yuppies, you couldn't throw a rope these days without lassoing a movie star, Jed thought wryly. But art teachers? They didn't make enough money to live around here.

Neither did he, come to that. If his foreman's job hadn't come with housing, Jed could never have afforded to stay on in the valley. As it was, he made enough to get by, but not enough to pay an art teacher! He shook his head at Felicity's well-meant but lamebrained notion and scooped more grease over the eggs, frying the tops without turning them over.

"It won't cost anything," Tuck said as if reading his mind. "You got an art teacher up your sleeve, do you?"

"Felicity does." He paused. "Brenna."

Grease spattered against Jed's hand. He didn't feel it. He didn't feel anything—except the shaft of cold white panic shooting straight through him, from his ears to his brain to his groin and straight on down to his toes.

"Brenna Jamison," Tuck clarified, as if there could be another. "You know her, don't you? Old Mr. Jamison's daughter. The artist from New York. Felicity asked her."

Tuck looked at him eagerly, but Jed didn't reply, just stood, riveted, the grease spattering on his hand.

"She said Brenna was an artist, not a teacher really," Tuck went on when Jed still didn't speak, "but that talent like mine should be encouraged—and, well, what did we have to lose?" Finally Tuck edged around so he could see his uncle. "You're burning those eggs!"

Jed moved at last. Jerked, really. Yanked his burned hand back, shaking it, scattering drops of hot grease everywhere, swearing under his breath.

Tuck jumped away. Jed scraped the eggs out of the pan and slapped them onto a plate. His hand was shaking. He flattened it on the countertop. Swallowed. Dragged a desperate breath up from his lungs.

"What happened?" Tuck demanded, watching his uncle worriedly.

"Nothin' happened." It was hard to even form the words. They were apparently unconvincing in any case.

Tuck's expression was concerned. "You okay? You sure?"

Jed gave him a hard look. Of course he was fine. It was the surprise, that was all. He took a deep breath, then another. And another.

Brenna. The name pounded in his head.

"So," Tuck said after a moment, apparently convinced now, his concern gone, his voice vibrating with cheerful little-boy eagerness again. "Brenna Jamison's gonna teach me! What do you think of that?"

"No," Jed said.

There was a moment of disbelieving silence. Then Tuck asked, "No? What do you mean, no?"

"Just no." Jed studied his fingers, then flexed them slowly. Calmly? Ha.

"But—"

Jed's head snapped around and he fixed his nephew with a glower. "I said no. You don't need art lessons!"

Tuck pressed his lips together in a tight line, looking exactly like Jed's kid sister, Marcy—Tuck's mother—had looked whenever someone had tried to stand in her way. "That don't make sense. You just said Felicity was right. And Brenna will teach me for nothin'. She told me so."

It was like a punch in the gut. "You *asked* her?"

"Felicity did, this afternoon, when Brenna came to school to see my stuff. She liked it. She said so," Tuck said firmly when Jed looked doubtful. "We're starting with drawing, 'cause I've done some already. I showed her when she dropped me off."

Jed's fingers sought the spatula, strangled it. "Dropped you off where?" A pause. *"Here?"*

"How was I gonna get home otherwise? I missed the bus. I figured you'd be out on the range. And here's where my drawings are." It was perfectly logical to Tuck.

"I was working in the barn," Jed said tightly, more to himself than to the boy. God, he could have walked out and run right into her!

If Tuck noticed the non sequitur, he didn't comment. "She didn't mind bringin' me. She wanted to see my drawings."

Jed licked suddenly parched lips. "You brought her in the house?"

Tuck blinked at his tone. "She isn't Madger the Badger, you know," he said, guessing wrongly what Jed's objection was. "She doesn't care how we live. Besides, we cleaned up good for Madger just th'other day. It doesn't look too bad yet."

"Madger the Badger" was Madge Bowen of some department of bureaucratic folderol. She'd been nosing around since last spring, sicced on them by some do-gooding yuppies who thought a hard-riding, tough-minded, simple-living cowboy was a questionable influence on a growing boy. Up until a minute ago she was the last person Jed ever wanted in his house nosing around. He hadn't considered Brenna a possibility.

"She liked my drawings." Tuck jerked his head toward the wall where they hung. "She said I had a lot of potential and she'd be pleased to teach me. So what do you think of that!"

Jed thought he was being sucked into quicksand. He glanced toward the spot above the table where he'd hung half a dozen of Tuck's pencil sketches of last spring's branding. They were framed in rough wood that he had knocked together not exactly professionally, and yet they were the best things in the room.

Brenna had been in this rough, bare room? She had seen not only the sketches, but the worn rug and sparse furnishings in the two-room cabin he and Tuck called home. Jed felt a hot curl of shame begin to burn inside him. Would she think he couldn't provide better than this? That he had nothing more to show for a dozen years than two rooms that didn't even belong to him?

"She didn't notice the house," Tuck was saying earnestly. "She isn't like Madger, pokin' her nose in everywhere. She just looked at my drawings. I wanted her to know she wouldn't be wastin' her time teachin' me. She's pretty famous, you know."

Jed knew. The whole damn valley knew. Hell, most of the Western art world knew all about talented artist Brenna Jamison. The pen-and-watercolor paintings she made of her Montana ranch heritage were famous far beyond the Shields Valley. In fact, they'd propelled her clear out of the state in which she'd been born. She'd gone away to art school eleven years before, and she hadn't been back—except for the occasional visit—until her old man had had a stroke in July.

Jed had heard she was here to stay.

He profoundly hoped not.

But according to Taggart, she was determined to take over at least until ol' Otis could run the place himself again.

"Got her work cut out for her," Taggart had said, shaking his head. "I don't think ol' Otis has been doing much in the way of running things for the last year or so. Can't see him bouncin' back."

It wasn't his business, so Jed had only grunted a reply then. He grunted again now. What Brenna Jamison did or didn't do wasn't any of his business. Except if it came to teaching Tuck!

"I gave her the ones I drew of you an' Taggart at the bull-riding school," Tuck was saying. "Remember them?"

Jed remembered. He often helped out at Taggart's bull-riding schools, running in the stock, doing a little bullfighting, keeping things moving, and usually Tuck came along and played with Taggart's daughter, Becky. But over the past year, maybe because he was growing out of playing with girls, Tuck had taken to watching the bull rides—and drawing what he saw. The sketches were wonderful. Quick, fluid sketches of animals and men in motion. In surprisingly few strokes Tuck seemed to be able to catch the tension, the intensity, the dirt and sweat and, sometimes, the blood.

There was one in particular, Jed remembered—of himself—when he'd let Noah and Taggart tease him into riding a bull again for the first time in at least five years.

"Like riding a bike," Taggart had said, grinning. "You don't forget."

Maybe not, but your reactions weren't all they used to be, either. And Jed had ended up on his butt in the dirt. Tuck had captured it deftly.

Jed used to get the sketch out and look at his own stunned expression every time he took it into his head to do something stupid. It had kept him on the straight and narrow pretty successfully over the past year.

Now he said, "You gave those sketches to *Brenna?* All of them?"

"She asked and I said sure."

"*I* didn't!"

Tuck's eyes widened. "They weren't your drawings."

"No, but—"

But I was in one of them, he thought, but didn't say. He tried to get a grip. Maybe Brenna wouldn't recognize him. Maybe she wouldn't care even if she did. Of course she wouldn't! Why should she? He didn't matter to her anymore. He was nothing more than a broken-down old cowpuncher from her past. Just because he'd once been fool enough to think he was man enough to marry her...

"What'sa matter with you?" Tuck demanded now, staring up at his uncle with unnervingly steady hazel eyes.

Jed wasn't going to win this battle and he knew it. Tuck was right; they were his drawings. Art was his talent. It was just that . . . damn it!

He braced his palms on the counter and slumped, letting his head drop forward. He shut his eyes and tried to think, tried to be clear and calm and dispassionate.

It wasn't working. It rarely did. That was why he needed the bull-riding sketch. So he had a visible reminder of what an ass he could make of himself, because he really wasn't the clear, calm, dispassionate type.

People thought he was, because he was quiet. They were wrong. He was quiet not because he was cool and dispassionate, but because if he didn't keep a lid on himself he'd blow sky-high. Like now.

"Nothing's the matter." He forced the words past his lips. He shoved his hand through his hair, then kneaded the knotted muscles at the back of his neck. *Nothing's the matter.* Maybe if he said it often enough . . .

"You won't have to stop work to take me or pick me up." Tuck was back at the art lessons, fielding objections before Jed could even voice them. "Felicity checked an' I can take the school bus that goes out by Brenna's ranch after school once a week. An' Brenna said she'd bring me home after."

Jed took a breath. "I won't be beholden to her. To anyone."

"We're already beholden . . . to everyone," Tuck pointed out logically. "How many times have you left me at Taggart's while you went away for the weekend? How many times have Tess and Felicity made us supper?"

Jed gritted his teeth. "When I go away for the weekend, I'm on Taggart's business buyin' cattle. You know that."

"All weekend?" Tuck's voice was mild, but his brows arched speculatively. He reached over and picked up the matchbook that lay on the counter by the stove. It said "Lucy's" in big red flowing letters and in smaller, equally red ones, "where the ladies are lookers."

Jed snatched it out of Tuck's hand and stuffed it into his pocket. He picked up the plate of eggs and shoved them at his nephew. "Your supper's gettin' cold."

Tuck took the plate, contemplated it, then set it back on the counter and made a face. "You have 'em. I'm sick of fried eggs. Anyway, I ate a roast beef sandwich at Brenna's."

It was the last straw.

Jed picked up the plate and crashed it into the sink, turned on his heel and stalked out of the cabin. He didn't bother to close the door.

It was the only bit of good judgment he showed. If he had shut it, they'd have heard the slam clear down in Elmer.

He didn't look like his uncle. He had red hair and freckles and hazel eyes that were warm and friendly. *He* was warm and friendly—like a puppy, eager to show off, eager to please. Eager to learn what famous artist Brenna Jamison had to teach him.

And famous artist Brenna Jamison had agreed to teach him, though she'd never taught anyone in her life—because Tuck McCall was talented, and he was determined, and he was enthusiastic. But most of all, let's face it, because he was all those things—*and* he didn't look like his uncle.

She was very much afraid that if he had resembled Jed, she would have been tempted to say no.

She couldn't have spent an afternoon a week, not to mention the occasional Saturday, in close proximity to a boy who was the spitting image of Jed McCall.

And what does that say about your maturity? she asked herself archly, as she prowled around the big old ranch house where she'd grown up.

It wasn't a question she wanted to answer. It was one that, up till now, she'd been grateful she hadn't had occasion to ask. In the two months she'd been back on the ranch, Brenna had glimpsed Jed only twice—and then just from a distance. Which was fine with her.

What would she say to him, anyway?

What did you say to a man who had said he wanted you, that he *loved* you, and then, the very next day, wouldn't even look at you, a man who had walked out of the room—and your life—without looking back?

There was nothing to say. Especially not now. And she was foolish to be fretting about it. Brenna was quite sure *he* wasn't fretting.

He probably didn't even remember she was alive, she thought, sinking into the old leather-covered armchair by the piano. It had been eleven years, after all, since their . . . since their . . . since their what?

Declarations of undying devotion?

Well, maybe hers had been. Clearly Jed's hadn't. To be honest, other than those words and the few kisses and feverish touches, which had never seemed enough, they hadn't had anything. Not by twentieth-century standards at least. And now it was almost the twenty-first.

At best she'd had an adolescent crush, and Jed had had . . . male hormones.

She didn't know what else to call it. He'd been twenty-one years old—at the height of his masculine urges—and, plain and simple, he'd had the urge for her.

At least until Cheree had come along.

Brenna closed her eyes. It did no good. The memory was burned into her mind: Cheree, the beautiful; Cheree, the worldly; Cheree, her brand-new stepsister, who had been everything that the unsophisticated, terminally naive Brenna had not.

The situation was so clichéd she would have laughed—if it hadn't hurt so much.

"What a man he is!" Cheree had said later, smiling knowingly. Brenna had wanted to die.

If she could find any consolation at all, it was that Jed hadn't married Cheree, either, though she was willing to bet he'd shared more than a few feverish kisses with Brenna's stepsister. Still, he obviously hadn't loved Cheree any more than he'd loved her.

Or anyone else, apparently.

Cheree had long since settled down and married a stuffy Philadelphia banker. But Jed was still a footloose bachelor at thirty-two.

Not that Brenna cared.

Not on your life. Brenna Jamison was well and truly inoculated against the likes of Jed McCall.

He could spout sweet nothings for hours on end and she'd turn a deaf ear. He could dance naked on a tabletop and she'd look away. He could—well, if he really did dance naked on a tabletop, she might peek. But purely for academic interest. She was an artist, after all. Human anatomy was grist for her mill.

Uh-huh.

Oh, Brenna, stop it, she counseled herself. She flung herself back up out of the chair and raked her fingers through her hair. Pins scattered across the floor as she shook out the dark auburn twist she'd anchored against the back of her head before she'd driven into town to meet Felicity and Tuck. Brenna shook her head, trying to relieve the pressure she'd felt all day. It was just because of her hair, she'd told herself. She'd pinned it too tight.

She knew better. It was because she might have seen Jed. She hadn't really expected him to show up after school at her meeting with Felicity and Tuck, and she'd breathed a sigh of relief when he hadn't.

But then, still playing with fire, she'd dared take Tuck home afterward. As she'd driven up the narrow track that led to the cabin where they lived, she'd spotted his truck parked by the barn, and her mouth had gone dry and her palms suddenly damp. The truck didn't mean he was there, of course. Chances were he was out on horseback, bringing in Jones's herd.

But he might not have been, and she knew it. He might actually have been there when she'd dared accompany Tuck into the house.

He hadn't been—thank God. What would she have said? *Remember me?*

Brenna pressed her palms against her heated cheeks. *Stop it,* she commanded herself once more. *It's over. Done. He wasn't there. And even if he had been, he's nothing more than a part of the past. You've got plenty of more important things to think about—and worry about—than Jed McCall.*

Like her nursing-home-bound father who was champing at the bit to get out of that "consarned prison," as he called it, and come back to the ranch. Like a ranch with eight hundred head of Simmental beef cattle that needed to be sorted and shipped within the next month with no one competent to manage it. Like the hands she had hired—Sonny and Buck—two of the sorriest excuses for cowboys she'd ever met.

Every other Saturday, which was to say after payday, Sonny and Buck went on a bender and were still so bent on Sunday night that unless Brenna went and got them, they never made it back to the ranch.

So far, every two weeks she'd done so, because they at least had a rudimentary knowledge of riding and roping, which was more than she could say for the ex-surfers that Job Service had sent out. Now there was a work ethic for you, she thought grimly.

So she was stuck with trying to keep Sonny and Buck sober until the cattle were sorted and shipped next month. After that she could breathe again—and start trying to get the rest of her life in order. God knew she needed to.

And to start once more to paint.

With the ranch, which hadn't had anything repaired in a year or more, from the look of things, and with running back and forth to Bozeman practically every few days to see her father, she'd been far too busy to give it a thought. She hadn't painted in a month.

She didn't even take a sketch pad with her when she went out riding anymore. Her artist's eye no longer sought the play of light and shadow, line and curve, but instead looked for signs of pinkeye and blackleg and scours. Loren, her agent, was getting impatient.

"It's all well and good," he'd said in his Eastern-boarding-school accent just last week, "for you to go back to Montana and dip into the well of your inspiration. You don't have to drown in it."

Brenna didn't want to drown in it, either. She wanted to make it a success, to prove that she really was the child of this land that she'd always believed she was. She wanted to show her father that she could do it. She wanted—needed—a future here. Not in New York.

"You want to *stay* there?" Loren had been aghast at the thought.

"Yes."

"But—"

"Don't try to understand," she'd said gently.

"Artists," he'd muttered. "Raving eccentric twits, all of them."

Brenna had smiled then. "Something like that," she murmured now.

But she would do it or die trying. Now, after two months of eighteen-hour days, she thought death might win.

It wouldn't, she vowed. It couldn't—because she needed the ranch for herself—and for her child.

That was what really kept her going, what kept her fighting, when by rights she should have given up long ago: she was going to have a child.

She pressed her hand against the curve of her abdomen, waiting, then smiling as she felt the stir of the child within. She always smiled whenever she felt those soft fluttery movements. They felt like butterfly wings. She remembered watching a pair of butterflies hovering near the geraniums on the terrace of their New York City apartment the day she and Neil, her husband, had found out she was pregnant. He had been thrilled. She had been scared to death. It was what she'd wanted, what she'd hoped and prayed for, and yet . . .

"They fly from here all the way to Mexico," Neil had said, his voice soft. "Yucatan, I think. Can you imagine that?"

"They don't all make it," Brenna had replied, preoccupied with her own fears.

Neil had smiled and shaken his head, then reached for her hands, pulling her down next to him on the lounger and looking deep into her worried eyes. "The strong ones do, Brenny," he'd assured her. "The strong ones do."

Brenna needed to believe she was a strong one now.

Neil had died in June. Her father had had a stroke in July. She was first a widow and now a rancher. And in three and a half months she was going to be a mother. She had her work cut out for her.

So why in heaven's name was she taking on another commitment—especially one with the last name of McCall?

Because art was in her heart, pain was in her veins, and another McCall had once been in her soul.

An exorcism then? Was that what she was hoping for?

She picked up the one sketch that had positively leapt out at her from the group Tuck had let her take home.

It was a rough drawing of a cowboy on his rear in the dirt, stunned by a fall from the bull in the background. In its untutored lines she saw resignation and determination. A man who had tackled something too strong, too big, too formidable to handle and knew it. A man who would—tomorrow or next week—do the same thing again.

Jed.

She hadn't seen him up close in almost a dozen years. She knew him in an instant, in a child's drawing.

At the sight, her fingers had clenched. Her stomach had twisted. Her heart had lurched—the way it always had whenever Jed McCall came into her range of vision.

For years she'd assured herself that Jed had been nothing more than a youthful infatuation—one she was well off never to have tested the limits of.

Oh, Brenna, you fool. The intensity of her reaction was enough to prove that she couldn't have been more wrong. The infatuation—if that was indeed what it was—had survived a dozen years.

An exorcism? Please, God, yes.

She was a successful artist. She had been a wife. She was going to be a mother. It was time—and she was woman enough at last—to face her unfinished business with Jed McCall.

Perversely the art lessons Jed couldn't prevent won him a point or two with nosy Madge.

"Well, good," she said when she came to visit and Tuck told her about them. "I'm glad to see your uncle recognizes your talent."

Tuck tactfully refrained from mentioning that his uncle's only contribution to the advent of art lessons had been his objections. "Oh, yeah," he said, grinning and giving Jed a significant look from beneath the red fringe of his hair.

Jed scowled. "Don't you have chores to do?"

Shrugging, Tuck took himself off to the barn.

When he'd gone, Madge looked at Jed over the tops of the half glasses that made her look like a nearsighted owl and ruffled her papers as if they were feathers. "Finally something positive I can tell them."

Jed supposed he should be glad one positive thing was coming out of the damned lessons, because sure as hell it wasn't his state of mind.

For the past three weeks he'd been treated to tales beginning, "Brenna says..." and "Brenna thinks..." and "When Brenna and I do thus-and-such..." more times than he wanted to count. It had been all he could do not to stuff cotton in his ears or a gag in Tuck's mouth.

Now they'd been at it four weeks, and when Tuesday afternoon arrived, Jed prepared himself for another onslaught.

He stood just inside the barn, out of sight, waiting for Brenna to drop Tuck off. He could've gone back to the house, but he didn't want to be walking across the yard when they arrived, and they were usually there by five-thirty.

But five-thirty had come and gone. Now it was past six. Jed prowled out from the barn and scanned the road, wondering where the hell they were.

"Madge would be proud," he muttered.

Madge's social worker heart was delighted to discover any paternal feelings Jed could muster up. He didn't know why she thought he was so damned deficient.

Hadn't he taken Tuck on when there was no one else at all?

When Marcy had died, he hadn't hesitated to take the boy, even though he didn't have the faintest notion how to raise a child. But they'd rubbed along okay, he and Tuck. It had been their bad luck for Tuck to miss the bus and be walking home in that damned winter storm and get picked up by a bunch of meddlers who believed in governmental solutions to family problems.

Jed ground his teeth the way he always did when he thought about it. Then he braced his hand against the doorjamb and squinted into the distance, hoping that glint was the reflection of the setting sun hitting Brenna's windshield as she wound her way up the hill. But the truck kept moving west and didn't turn onto the narrow track that led off the county road up into the hills where their cabin sat.

Six-twenty and still no Tuck.

Jed's fingers played with the cellular phone that hung from his belt. Then he shoved his hand into his pocket. No, damn it, he wasn't going to call. Tuck would turn up.

The phone's sudden ring sent him jumping almost out of his skin. He scrabbled with the case, wrenching the phone out and punching the button. "What?" he barked.

Over a line of static he heard Tuck say, "Can you come help?"

"What's wrong? Where are you?"

"At Brenna's," Tuck said cheerfully. "We were bringin' down some cattle. Then the truck died an' we tried to find Buck an' Sonny. But Buck's drunk an' we can't find Sonny an'—"

"Whoa," Jed said. "What cattle? What truck? *What about the damned art lessons?*"

Wasn't that what he was suffering through all this Brenna business for?

"We didn't get around to 'em today," Tuck said, unconcerned. "When I got here, Brenna was bringin' in some cattle. She said she'd stop, but I could tell she needed to be doin' the cattle more. She's shipping Friday and they ain't hardly brought any of 'em down."

"Haven't brought," Jed corrected. He might have said *ain't* himself in the not too distant past, but now he was a role model.

"So can you?"

"Can I what?"

"Come help," Tuck repeated impatiently.

Come help. Just like that. Jed shut his eyes.

"I figured you'd want to," Tuck added after a good thirty seconds of silence. "Not to be beholden an' all. An' because it's the neighborly thing." He quoted Jed's own words in far different circumstances.

It was, of course, but—

Help Brenna? *See* Brenna? *Talk* to Brenna? Oh God.

Jed worked his tongue loose, then swallowed, hoping for just a little spit so he could talk. "Just...fix the truck, you mean?"

"Well, maybe tomorrow you could bring down some cattle. If Buck's still drunk, I mean, an' she still can't find Sonny."

"I've got a job, you know."

"But Taggart's shipped already. He wouldn't mind. He'd prob'ly even help."

He probably would. And Taggart wouldn't feel near the desperation that Jed was feeling. "I'll call him," he offered.

"But you'll help, too," Tuck insisted. "You'll fix the truck, won't you? I told Brenna you would. Didn't you want me to?"

"No! I mean, yeah. Of course. I—" Jed dragged in a desperate breath "—I'm on my way."

It was just fixing a truck, he told himself, climbing into his own battered pickup. Nothing he hadn't done before. God knew he'd fixed this one often enough. As for the cattle...well, maybe Buck and Sonny—whoever the hell they were—would be back on the job by morning.

And if not...

If not—Jed shrugged tense shoulders against the worn seat of the pickup—he'd move the damn cattle. It was what he did every day, after all. Just his job. No big deal. Brenna being around wouldn't make a bit of difference.

It was pretty amazing the way a guy could lie to himself.

Two

"He's on his way." Tuck gave Brenna a confident grin, one that said quite clearly, *Everything will be all right now.*

Brenna thought she might throw up. "It wasn't necessary to phone your uncle, you know. I could call a mechanic and get the truck started. I could use my car to run you home."

"Jed doesn't mind. Besides, you'd still have to get those cattle down. Now you won't."

"What? Why?"

"Jed will get 'em."

Brenna sat down abruptly. "You asked your uncle to bring down my cattle?"

Tuck gave an innocent shrug. "Well, you need 'em down."

"Yes, but—" Would he think it was her idea? Would he think she was trying to get him back? Brenna's hands clenched into white-knuckled fists against the tops of her thighs.

Rational, she told herself. *Just be rational.*

"He's a good cowboy," Tuck assured her. "Don't worry."

"I wasn't . . . worried." Brenna drew a deep, careful breath, then let it out slowly. "I was just . . . surprised."

"Well, that's all right, then. I thought maybe you were gonna yammer on about bein' beholden, too. An' you aren't. This just evens things up."

Brenna blinked. "Beholden? Evens what up?"

"Oh, Jed was fussin' about me takin' art lessons from you on account of bein' beholden. An' he doesn't want us going to Tess and Noah's or Taggart and Felicity's for supper so often 'cause of bein' beholden," he recited. "So I told him if he was still worried about the lessons, this was a way of payin' you back."

"You told him that?" Brenna felt a little light-headed. She shouldn't have ridden so hard today. She should have eaten lunch. The doctor had said she shouldn't miss meals. Apparently the doctor was right.

"Yep. An' he's on his way," Tuck said cheerfully. "But maybe we still got time for you to show me that stuff about shading?" He looked at Brenna hopefully.

"Oh, oh . . . of course," Brenna said faintly. She latched on to the idea desperately. "Let's look at what you've done."

Tuck spread out his sketches. She tried to concentrate. Really she did. She took his pencil and drew a few lines to show him where the light was falling, then asked him where he thought the shadows would be. She might even have made sense. Tuck certainly didn't act as if she was babbling in a language he'd never heard.

He listened, nodded, then did as she suggested. At least she thought he did. Brenna wasn't sure. Despite her efforts to the contrary, she was listening every moment for Jed's truck.

At last she heard the rough sound of a truck engine laboring up the hill. Brenna straightened and licked her lips, waiting.

"Wha'sa matter?" Tuck asked.

She shook her head. Then she heard steps on the porch and a knock at the door. Her mouth went dry. She steadied herself with a hand on Tuck's chair back.

Tuck glanced up. "Want me to get it?"

"No. You finish your drawing." She rubbed her palms against the sides of her jeans on the way to the door, prepared to shake Jed McCall's hand with dry disinterest.

Sonny, the prodigal cowhand, stood there, one hand braced against the doorjamb, his hat shoved back and his chin thrust forward. If she'd thought Buck had cornered the booze market, she was mistaken. Sonny obviously owned a fair share.

"Where's m'saddle?" he demanded. "Who took m'saddle?"

"I haven't any idea," Brenna answered. A drunken cowboy was only slightly higher on her list of welcome arrivals than Jed McCall. "Where have you been?"

Sonny gave an expansive wave of his hand, teetered, and abruptly grabbed the doorjamb again. "Aroun'," he said with a hiccup. "Now'm back. Ready to work."

"Right," Brenna said dryly. "Go sleep it off, Sonny."

"Nope. Gonna work. Soon's I find m'saddle." He craned his neck and blinked blearily at her, then into the house. "There it is."

He lurched past her into the room toward the antique saddle her father kept on a stand near the bookcases.

"No, it's not." Brenna grabbed his arm. He would fall asleep on the sofa if he got within ten feet of it. She tried to redirect him. He teetered and flung his arm around her to remain straight up.

Brenna struggled beneath his weight. "Come on, Sonny. Back to the bunkhouse. We'll look for your saddle tomorrow. It's too late to work tonight, anyway. It's dark."

"Not too late," he slurred. He was fast becoming dead-weight. With his free hand he gave a shove and knocked the door shut. His head dropped against her shoulder and, a second later, he began to nuzzle. "Never too late," he mumbled. Then almost as though a new, more tantalizing thought occurred to him, he said, "'Specially not for this. You smell sweet, sugar."

Brenna tried to shove him away, but he only became heavier—and even more amorous. Now his lips were nibbling at her neck. "Sonny! Quit that!" She tried to twist away, but he was locked on now.

"C'mon, sugar..."

Tuck stood up to help her just as there was another knock at the door.

"Wha'zat?" Sonny muttered and wetly kissed her cheek.

"Oh hell," she muttered as Tuck opened the door.

Jed stood framed in the doorway as she and Sonny staggered past in their drunken two-step. Sonny's lips grazed her chin, his unshaven cheek rubbed her own. Brenna jerked her head back to avoid him and shoot Jed a glare at the same time.

"I don't suppose," she said to him acidly, as Sonny tried once more to kiss her lips, "you might like to cut in?"

In two strides Jed was across the floor to grab Sonny by the shirtfront, jerking him away and propelling him toward the door in one smooth movement.

"Hey! Leggo! I gotta get m'saddle. I come t'work."

"You wouldn't know work if it bit you on the ass," Jed said through his teeth. He gave Sonny a shove that sent the cowboy sprawling in the dirt. "Pack up your gear and get."

"No!" Brenna said, suddenly frantic. "He can't! I need him!"

Jed turned and stared at her.

She stopped and reddened, cursing cowboys in general and two in particular. "For the ranch," she said. "I need him for the ranch."

"You need help," Jed contradicted, "according to Tuck at least." He shut the door on Sonny and turned back to face her. "You don't need him."

Brenna saw red. It was his choice of words that did it—so close to those he'd used eleven years ago when he'd left her. *You don't need me,* he'd said to her then. Only the pronoun had changed.

And her life.

He hadn't changed. He was just the same, Brenna thought. Only more so. Leaner, harder, darker. More dangerous looking than he'd ever been. He stood quite motionless, and yet somehow she knew, as she always had, that he was not still.

The artist in Brenna understood *still.* It was a bowl of fruit, a pitcher of ale, a pair of shoes; an object there to reflect, not to act.

Jed, even motionless, exuded energy, tension, intensity. From the first sketch she'd made of him as a young man leaning against a porch railing in the moonlight, she had seen that. He might have looked quiet and unruffled on the surface, but Brenna had sensed even then the volcano of emotion that surged just beneath that implacable exterior.

The taut set of his shoulders, the tilt of his chin, the dark fire in his eyes told her that same tension simmered there even now.

"And you've always been such an authority on what I need," she said bitterly.

At her words the tension seemed almost to vibrate in him. A muscle in his jaw ticked. For a long moment he didn't speak, and she wondered if he was remembering his last words to her, as well. Not likely.

"Thank you for your concern," she said stiffly. "I can manage."

"Not with him."

"I make the decisions around here."

"You made a good one hirin' that guy." His tone was derisive. "Which is he, the drunk or the missing one?"

Obviously Tuck had elaborated on her personnel problems. "Sonny was the missing one," she said evenly. "He's not a bad worker when he's here."

"And sober?"

"He'll sober up," she said with more confidence than she felt.

"Not here."

"I told you, I need him."

"To gather cattle? Yeah, Tuck told me. I called Taggart. He and Mace and Noah Tanner and I will do it tomorrow."

It was the answer to a prayer and she declined it. "I won't be beholden," she began, remembering even as she did so that Tuck had said the same thing about Jed.

"You aren't. Consider it payment for the art lessons."

"The art lessons," Brenna said firmly, "are between Tuck and me."

"I'll help with the cattle, too," Tuck said quickly, his gaze flicking between the two of them apprehensively.

"You'll be in school," Jed said.

"After. I'll take the bus out here after. I gotta," he added. "Otherwise Madger'll show up and find me home alone."

Brenna didn't know who—or what—Madger was, but she saw Jed's jaw tighten convulsively.

He gave a jerk of a nod. "Fine."

It didn't sound fine, but Tuck didn't seem to care. "Come on," he said to Jed, "I'll show you where the truck is."

It took Brenna a moment to realize he meant her truck—the one that had died midway back from the pasture where they'd left the cattle. She hurried after them. "Don't worry about the truck."

"But it's dead," Tuck said.

"I can get it fixed."

"Jed'll do it."

Jed apparently intended to do just that. He was already in the driver's seat of his own truck. Tuck was climbing in the passenger side. Brenna huddled against the stiff north wind, watching them, feeling as if she was losing control, wondering if she'd ever had it in the first place.

"Aren'tcha comin'?" Tuck asked when she didn't move.

She shook her head.

"If that drunk comes back—" Jed began.

"I'll be fine," she said. Better than she would be going with him. He looked doubtful. "I'll lock the door."

Jed hesitated, then jerked his head down in apparent satisfaction. The truck shot out of the yard and down the road.

Brenna stood, arms hugging her chest, watching him go. A shiver shook her that had nothing to do with the cold. She took a deep breath and let it out slowly.

"There, see," she said aloud, her voice shaky, her words swallowed by the wind. "That wasn't so bad, was it?"

It was worse than he'd thought.

His reaction, that is. Her effect on him. Since he'd heard she was back he'd been telling himself that he was a fool to avoid her so completely, that surely after all this time he'd be immune. He was wrong.

If he'd been smart he'd have avoided her for another fifty years or so—until one or the other of them was cold and in a grave.

God knew he wasn't cold tonight. The mere sight of Brenna Jamison had heated his blood as nothing else had in years.

It was insane. What guy in his right mind could spend the past eleven years footloose and fancy-free and end up hot and bothered by a woman he'd walked away from in the first place?

Just one guy. Him.

"Damn it," he muttered under his breath, still breathing heavily now, hours later, as he slumped on the sofa in the cabin and dropped his head back against the wall.

By rights he ought to be cold and bone tired. He'd spent the entire day on the range. He'd spent the evening messing with Brenna's truck. He might have prided himself on having his own truck figured out, but his mechanical ability obviously ended there. If it hadn't, he'd have figured out a damn sight sooner what was wrong with hers: it was out of gas.

Simple. And yet, he hadn't had a siphon with him, so he'd had to drive home to get one. Tuck said he'd ask Brenna for one, but Jed vetoed that. He wasn't risking another encounter. By the time he came back and siphoned gas from his truck to hers, then followed Tuck, driving theirs while he drove Brenna's through the fields, it was well past nine.

He left Tuck to tell Brenna he had taken her truck to Elmer to fill the tank. By the time he got back it was ten. Tuck had eaten at Brenna's.

"She'll feed you, too," Tuck said airily.

But Jed declined, only stopping long enough to pick the boy up. Still it was after eleven when they got home.

It was past midnight now. He'd been up since five. He was bushed, all right.

But he wasn't cold. The heat of his reaction to Brenna was still warming him from head to toe—but most especially somewhere in between.

Damn it.

He yanked out a blanket and rolled himself in it on the sofa. He didn't sleep. The cold shower he'd taken once Tuck was in bed was just that—cold. It didn't soothe or settle or even distract.

In fact, it seemed to make things worse. It reminded him all too vividly of the showers he'd taken eleven years ago when what he'd really been aching to do was to take Brenna Jamison to bed. It was like being twenty again.

If he'd been hoping she'd have become frumpy and undesirable, he was out of luck. She'd hardly changed at all.

She was older, yes. She'd have to be twenty-nine now. But though she had matured, she'd lost none of the beauty that had attracted him since he was little more than a kid.

She still wore her hair long and waving down her back. He could remember weighing its silken heaviness in his hands, then running his fingers through it and rubbing his cheek against its glossy length. It was exactly the color of her father's Simmental cattle. Once he'd said so, and then had flushed with embarrassment when he'd realized he'd compared her to a cow.

Brenna hadn't cared. She'd laughed. ''My mother always said my hair was pure Irish setter.'' She'd tossed her head, and he could still remember the way the sunlight caught the dark copper highlights. It was the most beautiful hair Jed had ever seen. It still was.

And she was the most beautiful woman.

He'd always thought it funny that she should be an artist when, in his eyes, she was prettier than any model in any magazine he'd ever seen. But more than simple beauty, there had always been a gentle freshness about her.

When his family first moved to the valley he'd been fourteen and she'd been eleven. His father was little more than an itinerant cowpoke. Hers, he learned pretty quickly, was the richest rancher in the valley. Jed had thought a girl from her background would be stuck-up. But Brenna had never put on airs. She'd welcomed everyone into her world. Even him. In fact, she'd taken one look at the quiet, sober boy he'd been and had gone out of her way to make him smile. Unused to friendliness so freely bestowed, Jed hadn't known what to make of this girl who smiled at him and sometimes dared to tease him, and once during the brief time they were really dating, she had, God help him, given him a rose.

He'd taken a powerful lot of teasing for that rose, but he'd suffered it all in silence, because he knew why she'd given it to him. It was because he'd told her about the rosebush his mother had carried from place to place whenever they'd moved.

"We never had much," he'd said matter-of-factly. "We had the things that mattered."

"Roses?" Brenna had said the word not so much from disbelief as from enchantment. She had been lying on the grass, and she looked up to smile at him and Jed thought she was prettier than any rose he'd ever seen.

"Beauty," he'd said. "And honesty and faithfulness and keeping promises."

He remembered the words falling blithely from his lips. In those days he hadn't yet known the cost they would exact. Then he'd been young and full of life and hopes and dreams. Then he'd believed in his own strength, believed he had within him the things that mattered. And now...

Now he was a damn fool to be thinking about Brenna Jamison.

He tried not to. It didn't work. He wondered at the wisdom of New York men that no one had snatched her up years ago. Were their palates so jaded that they couldn't appreciate the refreshing beauty of her unadorned good looks? Surely there must be one among the millions who would want to fit her gentle curves snug against him, one would want to touch those smiling lips to his, one who would want those coltish legs wrapped tight around him in the night?

He groaned again. *Stop it,* he told himself. *Now.*

He didn't know what Brenna's curves were like these days. The oversize bulky sweater she'd worn had effectively camouflaged them from view.

Her lips hadn't smiled—not at him, anyway.

And her legs? Well, he'd only seen the outline of them in the narrow-legged denims she'd been wearing. But it had been enough to remind him of the times they'd stood so close that their bodies would rub together through his denim and hers. It had been sweet torture.

She'd always been so eager, so responsive, lifting her face to his like a flower opening to the sun. Wanting—and yet holding back at the same time, as anguished and as eager as he was, but determined.

Because whatever else she was, Brenna Jamison was a good girl. The marrying kind.

And a cowboy in possession of even minimal good sense knew you didn't trifle with the boss's daughter. You got up the guts to ask her to marry you first. You did things right.

Or you were Jed McCall.

Under the circumstances, though, he reminded himself, what he'd done wrong had saved Brenna a lifetime of misery.

It hadn't saved him. He'd felt the stab of self-doubt every day since. He deserved it, he told himself. It was justice. But, God, hadn't he paid off the debt yet? Was it only going to get worse?

He didn't see how it could get better now that she was back.

He was up before first light, wondering why, for all the sleep he'd got, he'd even bothered to go to bed. He loaded his horse into the trailer, then went back inside to shake Tuck awake and chivy the grumbling boy into his clothes and into the truck so he could drop him off at Taggart's on the way to Brenna's.

"It's not even six," Tuck complained as they bounced down the road.

"You're the one who wanted me to help with Jamison's cattle."

Tuck, remembering, sat up straighter. "Oh, yeah." He yawned mightily. "You sure I can't stay and help, too?"

"Over Madger's dead body. Felicity will take you in with Becky."

Tuck muttered under his breath, something about obstinate, stubborn uncles, but then sighed and slumped back against the seat. "Rather go with you."

And Jed would rather be anyplace else on earth.

Taggart and Mace and Noah, all of whom had agreed to help when he rang them last night, hadn't arrived yet when he got there. But in the rose-gray morning light he could see Brenna leading an already saddled horse out of the barn. She was bundled up in one of Otis's bulky old barn jackets. Jed didn't think it was all that cold, but maybe New York had thinned her blood. It was buttoned over a turtleneck sweater and hung halfway down her denim-clad thighs. Just as well, he thought. He didn't need a dose of Brenna Jamison's curves first thing in the morning. With luck he'd be well away before it got warm enough for her to take the jacket off.

She stopped next to his pickup as he shut off the engine.

"I didn't get to thank you last night," she said formally, "for the trouble you took with the truck."

"No problem." It was only half a lie. The truck, once he'd got his head together, hadn't been a problem at all.

"I didn't realize the gas gage was that unreliable. I feel like an idiot. And I appreciate it. I also appreciate your helping out today. I'd like to be able to say it isn't necessary. But I'm afraid it is. I couldn't do it with just Buck and Sonny."

He could see how hard it was for her to admit that. "I'm surprised you did any of it with Buck and Sonny," he said gruffly.

"They were all I could get." She smiled faintly. "The American cowboy is a dying breed."

Jed reached back to knead tight muscles in his neck. "Your daddy used to have some good men."

"*Used to* being the operative phrase. I'm sure you've heard he hasn't been exactly easy to work for lately."

There was no point in arguing about that. Always gruff and demanding, as he'd grown older and achier, Otis Jamison had given new meaning to the words *crabby old man*. In the past couple of years, even before the stroke, he had been a cantankerous boss.

Jed had been happy to take the job as Taggart's foreman when Mace had left, and not only because it meant he wouldn't risk running into Brenna on the rare occasions she came home. It also meant he wouldn't have to labor under Otis's steely gaze. He didn't know what the old man thought of him, but he was fairly sure it wasn't anything good.

You ought to be glad I didn't marry her, he'd wanted to shout at Otis more than once.

"How is he?" Jed asked now. He should have got out of the truck and started unloading his horse, but she was standing next to the door—so near he could smell the soap she'd used that morning, so close that if the wind gusted, it would blow her hair against his cheek. He drew a breath, held it, couldn't help savoring it—and stayed right where he was.

"Irascible," Brenna said. "Annoyed. *Annoying.* There's no one more irritable than a man in full possession of his wits and not of his body." She smiled wryly. "He wants out of the nursing home right this minute. He wants to come home, take charge, get back in the saddle."

"Any chance of that?"

"Not much. The stroke affected motor functions on the right side of his body. He's supposed to be doing therapy, but he has damned little patience for it. He may be able to come home when he can get around better, but at the rate he's going, that won't be soon." She sounded weary. Jed could well imagine that anyone who had to listen to Otis rant and rave would get weary pretty damn fast.

"Suffice to say, he's not a happy man," Brenna went on. "But at least so far, every time I go in to see him and he asks, 'How's the ranch? Are you taking care of the ranch?' I've been able to say everything's fine." She paused and stared at the rose-colored mountains in the distance. "I wouldn't be able to tell him that if the cattle weren't shipped."

"They will be." Jed glanced in his rearview mirror and saw two pairs of headlights heading their way. "Here comes the cavalry now. We'll have your cattle down before supper."

"Right." She drew herself together and said in a much stronger voice, "I was thinking two could take the north section. There's plenty up there that Buck never got to. One can do the creek drainage because we gathered most of those cattle already. And the other two can circle down south."

Jed was no dummy. He could do simple math in his head. "That's five," he said with a frown. "You're not countin' what's-his-name? Buck?"

"Buck's still hung over."

"Not Sonny."

"Sonny left."

"Then there's me, Taggart, Mace and Noah."

"And me," Brenna said.

"No, ma'am."

Brenna stared at him. "No, *ma'am?*"

He flushed, but kept his eyes straight ahead, not looking at her. "You want this job done today, we'll do it." Now he dared flick a glance her way. "But we don't have time to be baby-sittin' you."

"Baby-sit! You've never baby-sat me in my life, Jed Mc-Call!" The color was high in her cheeks, too. "Who do you think was helping Sonny and Buck! Who do you think was doing most of the work!"

"You, I reckon." He was willing enough to admit that. "And now you don't have to. None of us is drunk. None of us is missin'. We all know what we're doing. And we don't need any distractions."

Her eyes widened. "I'd distract you?"

Damn it all! That was what happened when he opened his mouth! He slammed his hand on the steering wheel. "You ride today, I quit."

The other two trucks pulled into the yard. Mace Nichols cut his engine. Noah Tanner, who had Taggart with him, did the same. They all piled out.

Brenna didn't even glance their way. She looked only at Jed. He could feel her eyes on him in exactly the same hurt, accusing way he'd felt them the day he'd told her she didn't need him, the day he'd walked away.

He wished to God he could walk away now.

But this time, this way, she did need him and he knew it. Jaw clenched, he stared straight ahead.

Finally she said, "Fine. Have it your way. Like I said, it's the ranch that matters." She paused, then added flatly, "I never realized you disliked me so much."

Three

Hell's bells! Was that what she thought? That he *disliked* her?

He stared after her as she hurriedly thanked Mace and Noah and Taggart, told them how much she appreciated their help, then brushed past them all as she led her gelding into the barn.

"Brenna? You okay?" Taggart called after her.

"Fine." But she didn't turn around, just kept right on going and disappeared into the barn.

"Whoa." Taggart raised his brows. "Who's she mad at?"

Jed got out of his truck. "Me."

Taggart looked at him accusingly. "What'd you do to her?"

Jed hunched his shoulders and headed toward the trailer to unload his horse. "Nothin'. I just told her we could do the work without her today."

All of them except Noah had known Brenna for years and so her reaction was no big surprise. In fact, Jed expected they'd argue with him on her behalf. He was surprised when they just shrugged.

"Probably just as well," Taggart said.

Mace, too, nodded his agreement. "Wouldn't want her to get hurt."

"Glad to see you agree with me," Jed said gruffly as he lead his horse out. "Now, here's the plan."

He outlined briefly the areas they needed to cover. Noah took the creek since he was least familiar with the lay of the land. Mace and Taggart would circle south. He kept the north section for himself because he knew the land. Besides, it was farthest, hardest and would be the best place to keep out of Brenna's way.

The others unloaded their horses and saddled up.

"See you later," Taggart said as he and Mace headed off. Noah touched the brim of his hat and headed toward the creek. Jed watched them go, holding his own horse by the bridle. The gelding sidestepped and tossed his head, eager to be on his way.

Jed was eager, too. But there was something he had to do first.

He went into the barn. His footsteps sounded hollow on the packed dirt, and he knew Brenna would be able to hear him coming. He could see her in the stall at the far end, still dealing with her own horse. She turned as he approached.

"Oh." She seemed startled. "It's you. I thought it would be Taggart."

"Taggart?" He frowned.

"I was rude to him just now." She bent over the hoof she held in her hand and went at it again with the pick.

"Yeah, well, he'll get over it." Jed hesitated. She didn't look up. "Taggart thinks you oughta stay here, too," he said, trying to justify himself.

Brenna kept scraping with the pick. She didn't reply.

"So do Mace and Noah."

Again, no response.

"Do you think *they* dislike you?"

Now she raised her head and looked at him past a fall of auburn hair. "No, I know they don't. What is it you're trying to say, Jed?" Her look of patient disinterest goaded him.

"That I don't dislike you, either, damn it!"

She gave him a bitter smile. "You always did have such a charming way with words." Then she turned back to the horse's hoof, making soothing noises as she did so.

"I didn't mean—I never meant—" Oh, hell. He sucked in a deep breath. "This isn't about now at all, is it?"

She lifted her head again, but she didn't answer, just looked at him.

He rubbed a hand against the back of his neck. Then he shook his head. "It wasn't you," he said. "I never disliked you."

Her indifference suddenly vanished. "But then *why*—?"

But Jed couldn't take any more. He couldn't explain. If she thought badly of him now, she'd only think worse if he tried to tell her what had happened.

"It wasn't you," he repeated firmly. "It was me." Then he turned on his heel and headed out of the barn, walking as quickly as he could.

It was me?

What on God's green earth did that mean?

And why did he just blurt it out, then take off as if all the hounds in hell were on his heels?

Brenna stood and stared, unmoving, until she heard Jed's horse canter away. Then, slowly, she went back outside in time to see his horse disappear over the rise toward the north.

"How was it 'you,' Jed McCall?" she murmured, intrigue and heartbeat quickening simultaneously. The baby kicked within her, as if it, too, were curious. Brenna patted her belly gently.

"Shall we find out?" she asked it softly.

She'd agreed not to herd cattle. She hadn't promised not to follow along and ask questions. She turned and headed back into the barn.

He should've known.

She might be sweet and smiling most of the time, but she was also the stubbornest, most determined little cuss he'd ever met. Why, he could remember clear back when she was twelve years old and he'd spotted her up in the tree spying on him and Taggart and Mace when they went skinny-dipping!

It was bad enough he hadn't discovered her until they were all three as bare as the day they were born. But then, after he'd dragged on his jeans again and confronted her from the bottom of the tree, demanding, "Get down outta there!" she'd merely giggled and stuck her tongue out at him.

"Make me," she'd said.

What fifteen-year-old boy could withstand that challenge?

He'd scrambled up the tree after her, moving quickly, threatening her at every limb. But she'd disappeared, and all he heard was her laughter floating back at him as she'd climbed higher.

She hadn't had the brains God gave a goose. Neither had he. Nor did either one of them know the slightest thing about backing down. So when Brenna went up, Jed went after her—farther and farther, higher and higher—until there was nowhere else to go, no limb that would safely hold her beyond the one she'd reached.

And that one turned out not to be safe either, when Jed reached it and began to shake it, too.

He could still remember the ominous crack, the tremble of the trunk under his bare feet, the wide-eyed startled look on Brenna's white face. He'd grabbed hold of her ankle when they'd started to fall. He didn't let go.

They tumbled in stages, hitting branches, breaking their fall, twisting, turning—scraped, cut and scratched. Then they hit the water. Or rather Jed did. Brenna had hit a rock as well.

She broke her arm. It was his fault.

They all knew it—he and Brenna, and Mace and Taggart who'd witnessed their fall. They took her home, trembling in their boots, waiting for the wrath of God and their fathers to come down on them when the truth was known.

But Brenna never said a word. Not a truthful one, anyway.

Jed had gone to see her three days later, expecting her father to tear him limb from limb. Instead Otis Jamison had pumped his hand and thanked him for doing his best to save his daughter from injury.

"What on earth did you tell him?" Jed demanded when he was alone with her. He was out of his depth as it was in the living room of the Jamisons' big, well-furnished ranch house. He didn't need to be confused as well.

"I told him that you caught me," she said matter-of-factly. "Well, you did," she said in the face of his slack-jawed astonishment. "You had hold of my ankle."

"Not tryin' to save you." Jed had to be honest even if it got him in trouble. "It was my fault you fell."

She shrugged. "Or mine for spying on you. It was worth it, though." She grinned irrepressibly. "You were very interesting."

Jed felt his face burn. He looked at her arm in its plaster cast and said feelingly, "Maybe you did deserve it."

Brenna had just looked up from the sofa and giggled, disconcerting him.

Seeing her riding after him now disconcerted him even more.

Jed hauled his horse around and reined in, glowering at her as she rode up. "I told you—"

"That you didn't want me working with you."

He scowled. "Right. So what do you think you're doing?"

"Finishing our discussion."

"We weren't having a discussion."

Not then. Not now. He touched his heels to his horse and moved on, hoping to leave her behind. Fat chance.

Her gelding kept pace easily. "You might not have been," she said. "I was."

He didn't respond. Discussions took two people.

"I've wondered for eleven years," she went on doggedly, "what I did to you to make you snub me that way. One minute I was your own true love—at least I thought I was. And the next you wouldn't even look at me on your way out the door. I racked my brains. Was I too forward? Did I throw myself at him? Was I too backward? Should I have gone to bed with him? Did Cheree do what I—"

"For Christ's sake!" Jed's explosion nearly sent his horse out from under him. He hauled the big gelding in and sucked a sharp breath of air. "I told you. You didn't do anything!"

"I know," she said. "It was you. So. . . what did you do?"

He clenched his teeth. He counted to ten. He counted to twenty. Hell, counting to a million wouldn't have helped. One more time opening his mouth got him in trouble. When would he ever learn?

He let out a harsh breath. "Just forget it."

"I don't want—"

"I do. It's over. And just because you're the big rancher's daughter, it doesn't mean you get everything you want." He spurred his horse on, kicking him into a lope, determined now to leave her in his dust.

She wouldn't be left. He rode on up the hillside, across the creek, up the draw. And every time he glanced over his shoulder, she was there, right behind him. He gritted his teeth and ignored her. Or tried to. He couldn't really. It hadn't been fair, what he'd said to her just then. She'd never pulled rank, never pretended her daddy's money entitled her to more than anyone else. So why had he said it?

Because he was a jerk. Because he needed all the defenses he could muster. Even if his defense consisted mainly of guilt.

She kept pace, watching his every move just the way she'd done when they were kids, dogging his every step, waiting for him to do something, say something, talk to her!

Well, he wouldn't.

He didn't have to. He'd just pretend she wasn't there.

Brenna, damn her, let him.

At the far reaches of the north section, he found half a dozen cattle up a draw and began moving them back down. One skirted around a clump of brush and got away from him. He could have used some help. He looked over at Brenna. She didn't move, obviously taking him at his word.

Jed cursed under his breath. He went after the damn animal himself. Brenna stayed where she was. When he got back, the other cattle were, surprisingly enough, still there. He gave her a narrow look which she met squarely. Though it wasn't obvious she was doing anything to keep them, he knew by the seemingly casual movements of her horse that she had.

He gave her a reluctant, quick jerk of his head, then made a clicking sound with his tongue and began to herd them all south. Brenna stayed back out of his way, still watching. Once he thought he saw a tiny smile playing about the corners of her mouth.

Mostly he tried not to look at her. It was a losing battle.

Then he tried to tell himself that all her years in the city had diminished her ability to ride. But that wasn't true either. She handled her horse very well. If she seemed a little awkward at times, it was probably because she was wearing that damned bulky jacket to protect her from the cold north wind. He didn't blame her for that. The wind was fierce.

He was just glad it wasn't snowing. Last year's October storm had stranded Taggart and Felicity overnight in Taggart's truck on their way back from Livingston. He and Brenna didn't need to be stranded together anywhere!

He worked without stopping, shadowed by Brenna, until mid-afternoon. Then, abruptly, she said, "I need to eat," rode over to a rock outcropping and dismounted.

Jed, startled at the sudden sound of her voice, looked over to see that her normally rosy cheeks, though wind bitten, looked deathly white. He couldn't help asking, "Are you all right?"

"Of course I'm all right. I'm just hungry." She didn't look up from where she was rummaging in her saddlebag.

Jed frowned, but shrugged, telling himself he ought to be glad if she was feeling the effects of being in the saddle. She should have stayed at the ranch like he'd told her to. He watched until she removed what looked like a lunch sack, then he moved off to look for more cattle. With luck, when he came back she'd be gone.

She wasn't. In fact she was perched on the rocks above the cattle, eating a sandwich and watching him ride in. When he got close enough he noted a bit more color in her cheeks. Swell. She'd probably stick with him for the rest of the day.

"Would you like a sandwich?" she asked. "I have roast beef and peanut butter and jelly."

Jed's stomach would have settled for either, since he'd forgotten to pack any this morning, but a sandwich would mean a conversation. "I'm not hungry. I'll keep working." He touched a rein to his horse's neck and headed east.

He took his time up the draw, found half a dozen cattle and moved them slowly back toward lower ground. Surely this time she'd have finished and headed home.

But when he came down, she was still there, sitting with her back to the wind, her collar turned up. She had finished her sandwiches, but she had the cap of a Thermos cradled in her hands and she was breathing deeply of the steam that rose off the liquid.

Jed's stomach, which hadn't quite forgiven him for declining the offer of a sandwich, growled again when he got close enough to smell the coffee.

"Want some? It's decaf."

"Wouldn't mind," he said. At least it was hot. He urged his horse close to the rocks and swung down out of the saddle. In the meantime Brenna had hauled herself to her feet and went to rummage through the saddlebag. She fished out a tin cup, then poured him some.

He was careful not to touch her as he took it and brought the cup to his lips. "Thanks."

"You're welcome." Up close he could see she still looked pale, but he suppressed the urge to tell her to go home. He knew better than to start another "discussion" he would lose control of. Instead he looked away, sipping the coffee, relishing the warmth as it slid down to his stomach. Out of the corner of his eye, he saw her shiver. His jaw tightened.

She took another swallow of her coffee. Her knuckles were white where she gripped the cup. "I think I'll head home," she said.

He stared at her.

Her lips weren't exactly blue with cold, but besides that paleness, he saw a hint of exhaustion in her eyes as she met his for just a moment, then looked away. She tossed the rest of her coffee on the ground.

Are you sick? he wanted to ask her. But he didn't. He stepped back as she bent awkwardly to pick up the Thermos, screwed the cap back on it and held it out to him.

"Keep it. There's plenty left. The sandwiches, too." She fished them out of the pocket of her jacket and gave them to him as well.

He took the Thermos and the sandwiches in nerveless fingers, his stomach blessing her even though he couldn't bring himself to say more than a curt "Thanks."

He stowed them in his saddlebag, intending to eat them as soon as she was on her way. He wouldn't give her the satisfaction of chowing down now. He swung into his saddle. "I . . . shouldn'ta said what I did," he said, knowing he owed her that much and a hell of a lot more. "About gettin' what you want."

She looked up at him. "No, you shouldn't have." She turned away and raised her foot halfway to the stirrup, then set it down again. She leaned against her horse.

Jed frowned. "What's wrong?"

She didn't answer. Deliberately she took hold of the stirrup and drew it out away from the horse, then lifted her leg again, gripped the horse's neck and started to haul herself up. She didn't make it. Jed stared.

"Brenna?" He was out of the saddle in an instant. "What's wrong?"

"Nothing. Nothing's wrong. I'm just . . . tired."

"Too tired to get on your horse?" He was incredulous. She might be out of shape, but they hadn't been going that hard. "Here," he said, modulating his tone slightly. "Let me help you."

He made a step with clasped hands and dropped it so she could put her foot in it. It was closer than he wanted to be to Brenna Jamison. It meant touching her, feeling the brush of her jacket against him as he lifted, letting her hair whip against his cheek. But if she really was *that* tired . . .

She set her boot in his gloved hands, took hold of the horse again and as he lifted, she lurched against him. There was more to Brenna than he remembered, a hard fullness where there should only have been soft down. He was so astonished he almost dropped her.

"*Brenna?*"

She stumbled against the horse. "What?"

"You're...pregnant?" He felt as though the world had just been knocked from under his feet.

He didn't need to see her nod to know it was true. Brenna? Pregnant? Hell, yes. And not just a little pregnant. *Very* pregnant. She had to be, else he wouldn't have felt the bulk beneath her jacket. His mind reeled.

Why hadn't he known? Why had no one said?

Surely she couldn't expect to keep it a secret? And people didn't anyway these days, did they? Bastards were accepted nowadays. He ought to know. Hadn't his sister kept Tuck?

Was that what Brenna was doing? Whose bastard was it?

All of a sudden Jed was furious.

"Whose is it?" he asked harshly. "Or do you even know?"

He had no right to ask, no reason to think she wouldn't know such a thing. But he couldn't help himself. They were questions born of a pain so intense he couldn't see straight.

She recoiled, looking at him, appalled, stricken. Her eyes widened and she held herself very still, her jaw rigid.

Then she said, "It's my husband's."

If it was possible for more of the world to crumble at his feet, with those words it did. *Husband? What husband?* Brenna was *married?*

"Your husband's?" He looked around as if the guy might be hiding in the brush. "So where is he?" Jed demanded when he found his voice at last. "Why isn't he out here helping round up the cattle?"

"Because he's dead."

Oh, God.

All the anger, all the fight, all the fury drained right out of him.

One look at her pale, stark face and he wanted to do something—anything—to take the bleakness out of her eyes, to put the color back in her cheeks. He opened his mouth, closed it, opened it again.

"Oh, Christ, Brenna," he said numbly. "I'm sorry."

"So am I."

They looked at each other then. His blue eyes searching her green ones.

At last she gave him a faint smile. "I'll survive," she said.

Something flickered in her eyes. A memory?

He wasn't sure. She turned and started to haul herself up on the horse again and, mindless, he boosted her. Once she settled in the saddle, she looked down at him with a clear green gaze. "I'm a survivor, Jed. Surely you knew that."

Then she turned her horse and rode away.

She was cold. So cold. And tired. Very tired. Exhausted. She'd overdone things. Been a fool.

So what else is new? Brenna asked herself as she sank into a tub of hot scented water.

Her teeth still chattered, her fingers trembled until she closed them into fists. She immersed herself and tried to get warm. It wasn't just the cold that bothered her, it was the tension. She felt as if her body was in knots, as if she'd curled around her child to protect it. Slowly, gradually, the water did its job. Her teeth stopped chattering, her shoulders slumped, and she slid down against the back of the tub. Her fingers floated aimlessly, curving lightly, no longer clenched in fists. She breathed deeply, slowly, and gradually her body warmed and eased. For the first time in hours, she began to relax.

As if it sensed the change, the baby within her stretched, too, then thumped and kicked.

Brenna laid a hand on her abdomen to feel the movement. It was less like butterflies today and more like someone moving furniture.

"Were you cold, too?" she asked it.

The doctor knew if it was a boy or a girl. So did the nurse. They had the results of the ultrasound she'd had taken in New York.

"Are you sure you don't want to know?" the nurse had asked Brenna the last time she was in Livingston. "It's more practical, you know—for buying clothes and things."

Of course it was. But no one had ever accused Brenna of being practical. If she'd been practical she never would have got pregnant in the first place.

Anyway, her child's sex didn't matter; it was part of the mystery. Her hand stroked the taut flesh of her belly, and the baby seemed to arch beneath her touch.

"Like that, do you?" she said and smiled. She hadn't had much to smile about lately—except this child. "I need to be more careful of you," she told it. "I shouldn't have gone after Jed today."

It had been foolishness right from the start. She should have listened to him when he'd told her not to come. But she had waited so long for any explanation from him, that, cryptic as those few words were, she couldn't let them pass. Not that she had anything to show for her pursuit—except a few hours of tormenting herself by watching Jed McCall.

"Your mother is hopeless," she told her unborn child. "Your father would despair of me."

That wasn't quite true. Neil had known all about Jed. And God bless him, he had loved her, anyway. So much that he had trusted her with the precious gift of his child even when they both knew he wouldn't see that child grow up.

He'd had a rare blood disease. By the time it was diagnosed, the outcome was, barring a miracle, a foregone conclusion. "I'm sorry I can't be more encouraging," the doctor had said.

He hadn't been the only one. The plans Neil Sorensen had made for his life—plans that included a wife, a family, as well as his already established career as a renowned sculptor—would be limited instead to his work.

Brenna remembered as if it were yesterday his reaction to that. They'd been standing in his studio looking at the stone sculptures that would survive him, and Neil had run his hands over them and then shaken his head.

"I thought it was important," he'd said. "I thought it was what mattered."

"It does matter," Brenna had assured him. He was her best friend, her mentor, the man she had looked to for emotional support practically since the moment she'd set foot in New York. She wasn't used to seeing him in despair.

"Yes, it matters," Neil had agreed. "But it isn't enough. It's beautiful. It's strong. It's a part of me. The strong part. But it's so cold." A shiver had run through him as he'd said the words. "I wish to God I had it in me to give the world more."

"More?" Brenna echoed.

His mouth twisted. "Flesh and blood."

She heard the ache in his voice, the wistfulness. And that was when her hand had stolen out to grasp his and she'd said, "Shall we have a child?"

He'd stared at her, astonished. But she'd seen a sudden spark of hope flare in his eyes. It was the first hope she'd seen in Neil since his diagnosis.

"A child?" He'd looked incredulous. "You'd have my child?"

"You wanted to marry me," Brenna reminded him. "You asked me often enough. Or was that a whim?" She gave him a mischievous smile.

"You know it wasn't a whim," Neil had said fiercely. "You didn't want to marry me!"

"I couldn't," she said.

Not when she thought that someday Neil might find the right woman for him. Not when she couldn't give him a whole heart. Not when a part of her—that foolish, foolish part of her—still, after all these years, longed for Jed.

But after Neil's diagnosis, it was different. Maybe under those circumstances, she *was* the right woman. He didn't seem to have time to find another he'd love more. And Jed? Well, Jed was a dream, a fantasy. It was time she grew up.

"I would be honored to marry you, Neil," she said softly.

"Are you sure? Marrying me means putting up with some bad months. And a child . . . It's a huge responsibility." He faltered, shook his head.

"Do you think I can do it?"

He studied her for a long moment, and she felt as if he was seeing to the very depths of her soul, gauging, assessing. Slowly he nodded. "Yes."

"I do, too, even though it won't be easy."

"It might not even happen. I might not be able…" His gaze had dropped.

She took his hand. "Whatever will be, will be." She gave his fingers a squeeze. "And if we have a child, I will love it for itself. But I will also love it for being a part of you."

His eyes had brimmed with unshed tears. "But is it fair?" he asked her. "To you? To the child?"

"Life isn't fair." Certainly by now they both knew that. Brenna put her arms around him and rested her head against his chest. "It's up to you."

"What about Jed?"

"Jed doesn't figure in this. Jed is past."

"He's still a part of you."

"Yes. But you're a part of me, too. I do love you, Neil. And I would love to have your child."

They were married the following week. They'd had six months together. They were some of the saddest—and happiest—moments of her life. They laughed, they cried. They worked, they played. And before he died, Neil finished all his projects, but one.

And that one would be finished in another twelve weeks—give or take a day or two.

Brenna smiled as she felt the baby kicking again in her belly. "You gave ol' Jed McCall a pretty big shock," she told it. "Good for you."

His brutal words and the sudden astonished anger on his face had shocked her. "Is that what you think? What do you care?" she'd wanted to lash at him.

But she'd been too cold, too tired—but mostly too afraid that instead of striking out at him in anger she might instead have burst into tears. She had done fine all day. She didn't want to betray her weakness to him then.

It was bad enough that she had to accept his help with the cattle. She would because without it she would have to give up, leave her father in the nursing home, sell the ranch, take her child and go back to the city.

She didn't want to have to do that.

The baby kicked her.

"You don't want to go, either, do you?" Brenna asked it. There was no answering kick. But there was life. A life that depended on her. Brenna drew a deep breath, tried to find courage, calm, faith in the future.

In her mind's eye she saw once more Jed's stricken look. She shoved it away.

It wasn't you, it was me. What had he meant?

Don't, she cautioned herself. Don't think about it. Don't think about him.

She wouldn't. *Couldn't.*

And yet . . .

"You didn't tell me she was pregnant!" Jed glowered at his nephew. He stalked from one end of the cabin to the other— not nearly far enough to wear out any of the irritation he felt. Hell, he could walk to New York City and still tackle every horse and bull that went to the NFR and still have enough irritation left over to wrestle a pack of bobcats single-handed.

Tuck looked up from his homework, his hazel eyes wide and guileless. "You didn't ask."

Jed strangled on the reply that sprang to his lips. He did another lap of the small room. "She should never have been out on a horse! And bringin' in cattle! She could have miscarried. Got herself hurt. Injured the baby!"

He didn't know why he cared so much. It wasn't his child. They weren't his responsibility, either one of them. It didn't seem to make a damn bit of difference. He banged his fist on the door. "What kind of idiot is she?"

"She's not an idiot." Tuck glared back at his uncle. "What'd you want her to do? Her dad's sick. He can't do the gatherin'. Buck and Sonny are always drunk or gone. They weren't doin' it. Nobody was till you and Mace and Taggart and Noah came. What was she s'posed to do, let the place go to hell?"

Madger would be washing both their mouths out for Tuck's language. Jed didn't even notice. He dragged in a deep breath and rubbed his hands down his face. There was no answer to that. Tuck was right; she had done the only thing she could do—save asking for help. And who would she ask?

Not him. He knew that well enough.

She could've asked Taggart or Mace for help. But until this week both of them had had their own cattle to get in.

Maybe once they were finished she would have asked. And maybe she wouldn't have.

She'd always been a proud little devil—even as a kid she wouldn't let anyone help her with anything if she could do it herself!

"What happened to her husband?"

Tuck shrugged. "Dunno."

Jed ground his teeth. He wanted answers, and he wasn't going to get them from his nephew. And he didn't know who he was going to get them from. Certainly not Brenna.

Did Taggart know?

Would he tell Jed if he did?

Taggart knew Jed had once been sweet on Brenna Jamison. He knew, too, that was all in the past. Would he think Jed was interested again if he started asking questions now?

"You're wearin' a hole in that rug," Tuck pointed out.

Jed slammed the door as he left.

He decided not to ask Taggart the next morning. After all, it didn't matter. Brenna wasn't his problem.

His resolve lasted all of an hour, until he caught up with Taggart in the bull pens near the barn. "You ever meet Brenna Jamison's husband?"

Taggart glanced up from checking over the bulls. "Nope. Gimme a hand here. We got a number three in with the ones." He was talking about the ranking of the bulls he used in his bull-riding school. Jed wanted to talk about Brenna.

"Who was he? D'you know?"

"Sculptor," Taggart said. He climbed the fence and jumped down into the empty central pen, then opened the gate to the one where the number three bull lurked.

Jed took a prod and climbed on the fence to poke at the bull. "What was his name?"

"Sorensen. Pretty famous guy, according to Felicity. I'm not much into sculpture myself." Taggart tried to encourage the bull to move through the gate as Jed prodded it.

"Famous, huh?" And an artist of sorts? Obviously a man who had a lot more in common with Brenna than he'd ever had. Jed's teeth came together. "How'd he die?"

"Got sick."

Jed made an exasperated sound.

Taggart shrugged. "You wanta know, why don't you ask her?"

Jed looked away. That wasn't even a possibility. After what he'd said to her, he didn't think she'd be speaking to him. He'd have to apologize. He shrugged irritably as if the hair shirt was already rubbing his back. "Don't matter. I'm just makin' conversation."

Taggart blinked. "You?"

Jed flushed and jabbed at the number three bull so hard he almost fell off the fence. It snorted, then trotted, at last, into the pen where Taggart waited. A quick closing of one gate and opening of another, some more judicious prodding and the bull was where he was supposed to be. Taggart nodded, pleased.

"On your way over this morning, you might stop and see if Howie Gilliam's got another roll of baling wire," he said.

Jed nodded and headed for his truck, then stopped. "On my way over where?"

"To Jamisons'."

Jed's eyes narrowed. "What makes you think I'm goin' to Jamisons'?"

Taggart grinned. "Aren't you?"

Four

He was only helping out because it was the neighborly thing to do. Because once upon a time he'd worked for Otis Jamison. Because he knew what to do.

Because there wasn't anyone else, damn it. That was all there was to it.

"What're you grinnin' about?" Jed grumbled when he showed up at Taggart's with the baling wire two days later.

"Nothing." Taggart hammered a nail in the loose board on the corral fence, keeping his eyes studiously on the spot in question. "Just wonderin' if you still worked here."

"'Course I work here. You don't see me for twenty-four hours, you think I'm loafing?"

"Well, I—"

"You want me, all you got to do is call." Jed thumped the baling wire into the back of Taggart's truck from his own. "You told me to go over to Jamisons'," he said accusingly.

"So I did," Taggart murmured. "Get the cattle down and sorted all right?"

"Almost."

"Want a hand with the shipping?"

"I imagine she will," Jed said stiffly. "It's not my herd."

Taggart smothered another grin. "I'll call and ask then. Are you helping?" he inquired politely.

Jed rummaged in the box of his truck and hauled out the cans of paint for the fence Taggart had ordered and which Jed had nearly forgotten. "Reckon so." He paused and glanced at the other man. "If you can spare me, that is."

"Oh, I think I can," Taggart said mildly. He squinted at the lumber in Jed's truck and frowned. "Howie send that wood?"

"I got it for Bren—it's the Jamisons'. There's a lot of loose wood on their porch." He'd practically fallen through it yesterday when he went to apologize. At Taggart's raised brows, Jed gave him a defiant look. "You want her to get hurt?"

Taggart spread his hands. "Of course not. I didn't realize there was a problem."

"There's a lot of problems," Jed said gruffly. And he was going to do what he could to fix them—to make amends for his big mouth. "I don't know that ol' Otis did a damn thing the last year or two. Place is goin' to hell. Somebody doesn't fix it up, it'll fall down around their ears."

"Good thing you noticed." Taggart smiled. There was something about his tone of voice that made Jed turn and look at him narrowly.

Taggart gave him an equable smile. "What?"

Jed muttered under his breath. "You want me to check on the bulls?"

Taggart shook his head. "I'll do it." He paused. "Maybe you oughta take the afternoon off. You been workin' pretty hard. Get some rest before shipping day."

Jed's eyes narrowed even more, but Taggart's expression gave nothing away, and if there was a twinkle in his eye, Jed couldn't see it.

"Maybe I will." He gave a quick nod and got back in his truck. "Tomorrow morning," he said as he flicked on the ignition. "Mackey says the trucks'll be there by seven."

"At Jamisons', you mean?"

"Of course at Jamisons'!"

"Right." Taggart grinned. "I'll call Brenna."

"Do that." Jed put the truck in gear and shot down the road.

Brenna told herself she'd get used to it—this sudden tendency of Jed McCall's to pop like a jack-in-the-box in and out of her life.

After his harsh words about her pregnancy the day she'd followed him on the range she thought she'd seen the last of him.

The next morning, though, it hadn't been Buck who'd turned up on her doorstep, or Taggart or Noah or Mace.

It had been Jed, standing there scowling at her.

Her heart had given a little lurch at the sight of him, but the rest of her hadn't felt welcoming at all. She'd tugged her robe a little more tightly around her. "What do you want?"

"To apologize. I shouldn't've said what I did ... about your baby's father." He'd shifted from one foot to the other. "It was a damn fool thing to say. I know you aren't that kind of woman." The color high in his cheeks, he'd ducked his head. "Sorry."

Then, without having given her time to reply, he'd skirted the rotten wood in the porch, taken a leap down the steps, got on his already saddled horse and ridden away in the direction of the cattle pens.

Brenna had stared after him, astonished.

But not more astonished than she was the following morning when she looked out to find him on his knees on her porch, pulling out pieces of rotten wood. With no preamble, not even a good-morning, he set to work replacing it.

She regarded him from behind a closed door, amazed. But then she decided that he'd told Taggart about the porch and Taggart had sent him over to fix it. She rang Taggart to thank him.

Taggart didn't seem to know what she was talking about. "Jed's fixing your porch? Well, good for him, I wondered where he was."

Brenna frowned as she watched Jed through the window, still hammering. "I thought you knew," she said. "I didn't realize it wasn't your idea. If you want him back..."

But Taggart quickly declined. "He ain't worth a lick around here at the moment," he said, then coughed and changed it to, "I mean, I got things pretty squared away. You're welcome to him."

Just then Jed hit his fingers with the hammer and swore mightily. Brenna stifled a smile, but it faded and her expression grew perplexed as she watched him. Was this his way of making amends? Probably. Jed was honorable to the teeth.

She wanted to tell him not to bother, but damn it, the porch needed seeing to, and if his guilty conscience got it done, well, she'd just grit her teeth and accept it.

So while she did the laundry and the mending and continued her efforts to get the house back up to snuff, Jed finished the porch, then he left again.

Shortly after noon, he was back, dusty and sweaty.

"Gotta talk to your father," he said without preamble. "I've been sortin' and shapin' up your cattle but it's been a couple years since I've seen 'em. I need to know more."

"I'll call him." She opened the door wider. "Come in."

Jed looked as if he was about to decline, but then nodded and brushed past her into the kitchen.

Brenna's hands twisted. "Thank you...for fixing the porch."

"Needed to be done."

"Yes, but you didn't need to do it." She sighed at the sight of his jaw tightening. "Thank you," she repeated. "Would you like something to eat? Sit down at least."

He shook his head. "Just want to talk to your father." He stayed right where he was, looking at the phone on the wall, not at her.

Brenna dialed the number. When she had her father on the phone, she handed it to Jed and went back to her mending.

The conversation—both sides she was sure, though she heard only one—was terse and technical. How ranch men could talk shorthand about particular steers in a herd of several hundred who all basically looked alike had never ceased to amaze her.

She had an artist's eye for detail, but the finer points of each particular bovine somehow escaped her.

Jed made notes on a small pad of paper he took from his vest pocket. He chewed the eraser of his pencil while Otis talked, then made more notes, grunted, wrote some more.

"Got it," he said finally, then paused, listening to whatever Otis was saying. Then he said, "No big deal. Reckon you'd do the same for me, sir." He hung up and headed for the door.

"Thanks," he said over his shoulder. And he was gone again.

Brenna saw him once more that evening when he was loading his horse in the trailer. She went out to tell him that Mackey Vance had called and said he'd have the trucks there at seven in the morning. She felt awkward doing it, as if she were presuming too much; as if she were pressuring him when she had no right.

But he nodded. "I'll be here."

He and Taggart, Mace and Noah arrived well before Mackey showed up the following morning.

Brenna went out to meet them in the yard, to thank them for coming, to offer her help.

"You set one foot outta that house today and I'll quit and take them all with me," Jed said, jerking his head in the direction of the other men. He leveled a gaze at Brenna. "Just in case you're thinking about it."

Taggart grinned. "Better listen to him, Bren."

Brenna bristled. Her cheeks flushed and she scowled at Jed. He looked back at her implacably. Their eyes dueled. The baby kicked and Brenna's gaze dropped. There wasn't any question about who was going to win.

"Have it your way," she conceded with ill grace. "I'll get everyone dinner."

"Tess and Felicity and Jenny will bring dinner."

"Tess and Felicity and Jenny are welcome to come. But I'm cooking," Brenna said, her voice every bit as firm as Jed's. She looked at him defiantly. "And if you want to stop me, you'll have to spend the day in the house, not out with the cattle."

Taggart laughed.

This time it was Jed who huffed and looked away. "Damn stubborn woman," he muttered as he turned to unload his horse.

"You'd better believe it," Brenna said loud enough for him to hear.

Then she turned on her heel and went into the house. She cooked for most of the day.

Tuck arrived on the school bus, and she saw him head straight to where the trucks were loading cattle. Ten minutes later he reappeared, grumbling.

"He said I was in the way," he groused.

Brenna didn't ask who "he" was. She knew. "Your uncle doesn't seem to want much help. He chased me off this morning."

"Well, you're a girl."

Brenna raised her brows. "They're my cattle."

"Yeah, well . . ." Tuck shook his head.

"Come have some chocolate cake and a glass of milk."

Complaints forgotten, Tuck chowed right down.

Feeding Tuck McCall had become something of a habit. The first time he'd come for a lesson, she'd offered him a plate of sandwiches and cookies a little hesitantly, not quite sure what growing boys liked. It turned out they liked anything—and a lot of it. He ate everything she prepared, and now Brenna fed him every time he came.

Today he ate two pieces of chocolate cake and a ham sandwich before he went out in the yard with his sketch pad and a ball to toss to her father's dog, Trout.

"Find something interesting," Brenna told him. "Draw it and we'll take a look at it later."

She was just putting the potatoes on when Felicity and Tess arrived with four children and casseroles and plates and baskets of food in tow.

Becky and Susannah, who were Tuck's age, unloaded the dishes they'd brought, said hi to Brenna and disappeared back outside to play with him. Tess settled her little ones on the floor with toys she'd brought while Felicity put even more dishes of food on the table. A few minutes later Mace Nichols's wife, Jenny, arrived bearing a cake and a big bowl of chili.

"I can see I didn't need to bring a thing," she said, eyeing the table full of food Brenna had already prepared.

"It was the least I could do—all Jed would let me do," she grumbled.

Felicity and Tess exchanged a glance.

"Jed's a little smitten," Felicity said with a smile.

"Just a little," Tess agreed.

"No," Brenna said flatly, "he isn't."

At her tone, Felicity and Tess blinked.

But Jenny said quietly, "He was once, wasn't he?" She was the only one of the three to have grown up around here, but she was older than Brenna, and Brenna had hoped she wouldn't remember.

"We dated," she allowed, turning her back and opening the oven to take out the lasagna she was baking. "For a short time."

The other women exchanged another look. "Ah," Jenny said knowledgeably.

Brenna fixed her with a hard look. "It's been over for years."

They all nodded solemnly. Self-conscious under their combined gazes, Brenna turned back to the oven. Its heat seemed preferable to letting them see the tear in her heart that Jed McCall had made when he'd left her.

"Let me take that!" Tess whisked the lasagna pan out of Brenna's hands the moment she retrieved it. "You don't want to lift heavy things in your condition."

"You should be sitting down," Felicity told her sternly. "You've been working flat out all day."

"You can keep an eye on the trolls—" Tess nodded in the direction of Clay and Scott who had abandoned the toys they knew for the unfamiliar attraction of Brenna's pots and pans. "When they draw blood or the guys come in—whichever happens first—you can get up. In the meantime, relax."

Because Jenny literally pushed her down into a chair and because they showed no qualms about taking over completely,

Brenna sat. She didn't want to. She'd felt keyed up and restless all day, unwilling to sit still.

But now, with the bustle and gentle conversation of the other women around her and the little boys playing on the rug in front of her, something in her began to ease. For the first time in months she didn't feel so alone, so embattled. A sigh escaped her.

The baby lurched. She put a hand on her abdomen.

"Waking up, is he?" Tess asked. "I remember Scott used to wait until I sat down and then he'd really kick. Hard to believe looking at him that it was just a year ago."

And Brenna, watching Clay and Scott now, marveled at the notion that in a year her own child might be sitting on this floor banging on a lid with a spoon.

"They grow up so quickly and change so fast. Even the big kids. You can't believe how Tuck has blossomed since you've been teaching him." Felicity smiled at her. "Nelda Jacobs, his teacher, can't believe the change. She was worried about him before, said he seemed reclusive, distracted. And now he's a different child."

"I'm sure it isn't all because of his art lessons."

"Not all, but mostly. He needed that opportunity. And Jed certainly couldn't give it to him. I don't mean he begrudges Tuck his talent," Felicity said. "He just doesn't have the time—or the knowledge."

"I suppose not," Brenna agreed quietly. But he did have the appreciation. He used to love to watch her work. He'd sit next to her, unmoving for hours, just watching her pencil move over the page.

At first she'd been self-conscious about it, but he'd said, "Hey, you watch me rope, don't you? Same thing." She wasn't sure about that, but she understood what he meant. Jed had always appreciated competence. He appreciated talent. She bet he watched Tuck draw.

When he did, did he ever think of her?

There was a sudden wail from the boys on the floor. Clay had clopped Scott on the head with a lid.

"Oh, dear!" Brenna started to struggle up out of the chair.

"I'll get him." Jenny stooped to gather Scott into her arms as Tess hurried over.

"Maybe we should stop playing pots and pans," she suggested, comforting him.

"Come on, Clay," Felicity said. "I'll read you a story." She scooped Clay up and carried him into the living room. Tess, still holding Scott, followed.

"Felicity's right, you know," Jenny said to Brenna when the other two women had gone. "I work as an aide and I've seen Tuck in class. The art lessons have really made a difference. They've helped him develop, become more the person he wants to become."

"I'm glad."

"You've helped Jed, too."

"Helped Jed? How?"

"The department of children's services—or whatever it's called these days—has been snooping around, checking on him. And Tuck."

Brenna stared at her. "Checking on Jed and Tuck? Why?"

"They're worried that Jed isn't the best guardian, that Tuck's needs aren't being met."

"That's ridiculous." Brenna might not be one of Jed McCall's biggest fans, but there was no doubt he would do anything for Tuck—even if it meant letting him take art lessons from her!

"You know that, and I know that. But, well, Jed isn't exactly Mr. Affability. He never goes out of his way to make anyone like him. Including the bureaucrats who come nosing around." Jenny shook her head despairingly. "And he isn't exactly your conventional parent."

"No." Brenna could see that. "But surely they don't think Tuck is neglected."

"Who knows what they think. But from what Madge—that's the social worker—said, Tuck's art lessons are a plus. It makes them think Jed is paying attention."

"Of course he is." He always paid attention. He might not be conventional, but he was always responsible. Just look at the new boards in her porch. He probably even thought he was being responsible eleven years ago when he walked out on her. Once he'd fallen head over heels for Cheree, he hadn't wasted a moment pretending he was still in love with her.

He could have told her why, she argued with herself. But she knew he wouldn't, because he wouldn't want to hurt her. Little did he know!

"Well, if you see Madge, tell her so," Jenny said. "Jed will be forever grateful."

"They're comin'!" Tuck banged open the door. "They're all loaded up and comin' this way!"

Brenna struggled to her feet and went to watch as the first truck came over the rise and rumbled down the gravel road past the lane that led up to the house.

One after another, they came and they went—taking with them her hopes for the ranch—for her father, for her child, for herself.

A few minutes later came the men who had made it possible. Mace and Noah and Taggart piled out of the first pickup, grinning and laughing.

Jed arrived alone in the second. He got out of his pickup and wiped a hand across his forehead. Mace said something to him. He grinned, too. Then he looked after the trucks and, when they disappeared, his gaze turned toward the house.

Once Brenna had dreamed of seeing him like this: hot, dirty and tired, yes, but very much a part of this ranch, of her life.

Eleven years ago—on the night after shipping—that dream had begun to fall apart.

And now?

Now he was back. Awkward, silent, gruff. Nearly as shy as he'd been as a boy, when he'd first been smitten.

Tess and Felicity thought he still was. Could he possibly...

No. He couldn't.

She was insane to think it. But something deep inside Brenna sparked to life at the possibility. Something long buried flickered, flared.

She looked at the man who pulled off his hat and rubbed a bandanna down his face. The man who had walked out on her without an explanation eleven years ago and yet who came to her rescue now, taking charge, helping out, seeing that everything was done, large or small.

It wasn't you. It was me.

Dared she hope . . . ?

"Oh, Brenna, be careful what you pray for," she murmured and shut her eyes.

He didn't want this.

The warm, cozy room, the sounds of laughter, friendship, camaraderie. The giggle of children, the crackle of the wood fire, the tired, pleasantly full feeling that came with a good meal after a hard day's work. He didn't want any of it, Jed thought, as he braced himself against the hearth.

He wanted a cold night, a hard narrow bed, sleep. And no dreams. Please, God, no dreams—especially not dreams of the reality crossing his field of vision at this very moment, as Brenna trundled across the room, her auburn hair loose about her face as she went, her body gorgeous even as it was ungainly. Full with another man's child.

The piece of kindling in his hands snapped with a loud crack. No one noticed.

He wasn't surprised. Noah and Taggart, at ease and replete, were taking turns telling stories about awesome, rough stock rides they'd made. The kids, who were sprawled around them on the floor, listened with rapt attention, their jaws slack, their eyes wide. The women were smiling, encouraging, laughing at their stories—oohing and ahhing in all the right places. Even Brenna. Especially Brenna.

All evening long he'd felt her eyes on him, quick questioning glances that raised the hair on the back of his neck. Even now as she was curled at the end of the sofa, she looked at him from beneath lowered lids. He looked away. But he could still see her toes peeking out from beneath a sort of soft, colorful robelike thing she was wearing. Felicity called it "a caftan," so he guessed that's what it was. It made her look sexy and desirable as hell and—

Jed shoved himself to his feet. "C'mon, Tuck. Let's go." His voice was loud and harsh, breaking into Taggart's story. A startled silence filled the room.

Tuck stared up at him. "Go?"

"Go," Jed repeated. He dug a toe under his nephew's rear end. "Gotta get up early in the morning." It was his don't-argue-with-me tone.

No one said a word. Everyone's eyes were on him. The room grew hot and close the longer he stood there. He needed air. Cold air. And lots of it. Now. He fixed Tuck with a steely look. "I said, let's go."

For a long moment Tuck didn't move and Jed wondered if he was going to have his authority challenged tonight. If there was ever a time he didn't need that, this was it. Something in his gaze must have got the message through to Tuck because the boy sighed and hauled himself slowly to his feet.

"Get your jacket."

Jed waited until Tuck had headed toward the closet, then he turned to Brenna and gave her a sharp nod. "Thanks for the meal."

She hauled herself to her feet. Her cheeks were rosy from the fire and from her laughter. She looked as beautiful as he could ever remember.

"I should be thanking you."

"You already did," he said gruffly. More than once. In that same soft voice he remembered all too well—the one that could melt him and harden him at the very same time.

"I'll never be able to say it enough." And as she said the words, he saw her hand come up as if to reach out to him.

God, no! he begged silently and was relieved when she suddenly looked self-conscious. She pulled back woodenly, and her hand dropped to her side. A mask of politeness covered the flicker of hurt he saw cross her face.

Tuck reappeared, shoving his arms into his jacket, looking disgruntled.

Jed didn't care. He gave the boy a light push toward the door. "Say thank you for the meal."

"Thank you for the meal," Tuck said like a robot. Jed wanted to strangle him. Then the boy grinned at Brenna. "It was super. Really. Lots better'n we get at home." He flashed Jed a defiant look and shot out the door toward the truck.

The kid understood all about self-preservation. If Jed was going to strangle him, he'd have to catch him first.

He got drunk as a skunk in a funk.

All the cold air and narrow, hard beds in the world hadn't done a damn bit of good at all. Brenna Jamison was right in there with him. He tossed and turned and thumped and muttered to no avail at all.

He was grateful Tuck was a sound sleeper. The boy never heard him get up and hit the whiskey bottle. Never heard him pour one glass. And then another. He never heard Jed slam the glass against the countertop so hard it broke. He never heard the bottle fall empty onto the floor or Jed kick it under the table.

And Jed never heard him, either, when he got up the next morning and left for God knew where.

He groaned now and considered sitting up, then thought better of it. It was late—damn late. The sun was straight up in the sky. To a man who got up before the sun every morning, it seemed as if he'd lost the entire day.

He wished he had, if the start was any indication of how the rest of the day was going to go. His head felt like a herd of cattle was stampeding through it. He rubbed a hand experimentally down his face. Even his whiskers hurt. He ran his tongue over parched lips. His mouth tasted vile.

He hadn't been this hung over since—a shudder ran through him—since he'd walked out of Brenna Jamison's life.

Which was, he thought sourly, why he was hung over again now.

Last night at Jamisons' ranch had reminded him all too forcibly of the last evening eleven years ago when they'd been a couple.

That night had followed a shipping, too.

He'd eaten dinner in that very same house, laughing, smiling, appreciating the warmth, the camaraderie, the satisfaction of a job well done. He'd sat on that very couch, watched logs burn in that same fireplace. That night, though, he'd had his arm over Brenna's shoulders. He'd had her warm body pressed snugly into his side, and whenever she'd turned her head, she'd brushed her lips across his cheek and smiled at him. In her eyes he'd seen the promise of things to come.

He groaned now and pressed his fists against his eyes. His head was pounding. His body was hard, stiff with need, taut with desire. He ached with it.

A knock on the door made his head jerk up. He cursed as the cerebral cattle started stampeding. "Damn!"

Holding his head in his hands, he eased himself up slowly, carefully. Another knock came, sharper and more insistent than the first.

"'M comin'. Whozit?" he croaked. He hobbled across the room and jerked open the door.

Madge Bowen's eyes widened at the sight of him, unshaven, uncombed, undressed except for a pair of unzipped Wranglers.

"Oh, God." His own eyes shut. He groaned as he scrabbled to zip up his jeans. Madge sucked in a sharp, disapproving breath.

He wished he could close the door on her. He would've if he'd been able to, but his alcohol-soaked reflexes weren't sharp enough. He wasn't that quick. Madge pushed past him into the room and thumped her briefcase on the table. He winced.

She regarded him unsympathetically. "Get dressed."

He didn't move. Couldn't have if his life had depended on it. "Go 'way."

"I can't. It's my job to be here."

"Not t'day. It's Saturday."

"Today," she said firmly. "Today more than any other day from the looks of things. Get dressed, Jed. We need to talk."

He couldn't fight her. And God knew he wasn't going to be able to move her. Damn Madge Bowen! She was more trouble than any balky steer he'd ever run across. Summoning every bit of strength he had, muttering under his breath, he padded past her toward the bedroom. Behind him he heard Madge make a noise that combined dismay and disgust.

He got dressed. He ducked his pounding head under the faucet. He shaved and combed his hair while he was at it. He didn't know precisely why Madge was there, but it looked official. And whatever it was, he doubted that looking like road kill was going to help his cause any.

Studying his bloodshot eyes in the mottled bathroom mirror, he wasn't sure anything was going to help his cause.

Better get it over with while he still had a little alcohol in his system to dull the pain. Sucking in his breath, Jed went out to face the music.

Madge had made coffee. She had also cleaned up the broken glass.

As he came into the room, she swept it into a paper bag, rolled it up and put it in the trash. Then, turning her back to him, she wiped down the countertop with the smooth efficiency of long practice. She had done the dishes, too. And the whiskey bottle was no longer under the table.

He grunted an acknowledgment. He thought she might take it as "thanks."

Now, as he stood there in his socks, she poured a cup of coffee and thrust it into his hands.

He cradled it carefully, sniffing the strong aroma, wondering how it would react to the whiskey in his gut if he took a sip. He didn't have high hopes.

Madge looked him over from the top of his ruthlessly tamed hair to the hole he was trying to edge out of sight beneath the toe of his left sock. He doubted a marine corps drill sergeant had a more assessing stare.

"Better," she said. She didn't have to say, *But not by much.* She sat down. Jed, grateful, because he might have fallen over if he'd had to stand much longer, sat across the table from her. He put the cup in front of him with careful precision, keeping his fingers curled around it, as if it would keep him anchored.

Madge opened her briefcase and pulled out a folder of papers. She laid it on the table, then pulled out an official-looking document.

"I shouldn't even be here today because, as you point out, it is Saturday. But I wanted you to see this. To think about it." She shoved it across the table.

"What is it?"

"A petition to have your custody revoked." She turned it and spread it on the table so he could read it. "A preliminary petition. A rough draft, if you will. I got it in the mail this morning."

Jed thought he might throw up. His fingers tightened so hard around the mug he thought it might shatter in his grip. He clamped his teeth shut against the bile that rose in his throat.

He bowed his head. Not to read the petition. He didn't need to read it. He could guess what it said.

"No comment?" Madge said quietly after an eternity.

Jed let out what was left of a shaky breath. But it was still a long moment before he lifted his head and met her gaze.

The starch was gone from her expression now. She looked concerned, motherly—though it had been so long since he'd had a mother he couldn't be quite sure. "Do you want to give Tuck up, Jed?" she asked almost gently.

"No!" The word exploded from him. His head felt as if it might split. He pressed it together with his hands, then dragged them down his face and laced them together, propping his elbows on the tabletop and staring at Madge over his knotted fingers.

"No," he said again, his voice softer but even more ragged. "I want to keep him."

"Well, today's little scenario isn't the way to do it." She was still looking at him kindly, but her words were blunt.

He sighed and dragged his fingers through his hair. "I know that. It was—" He groped for words to explain. There were none. "Yesterday was a long day," he said at last. Eleven years long, it seemed.

"I was shot. Couldn't sleep." He rubbed his fists against his mouth. "No excuses." He lifted his eyes and met her gaze as steadily as he could.

"There are no excuses," Madge said firmly. "None that the department will accept, anyway. You can't let this happen again, Jed."

"It won't."

They looked at each other. Finally Madge picked up the papers and slipped them back in a folder, then she looked at him again. "I don't want to have to make a final draft of this, Jed."

"You won't have to," he swore.

Madge glanced around the small room. Her eyes seemed to linger longer than Jed would have liked on the corner in which he'd kicked the whiskey bottle. Slowly her gaze came back to rest on him.

"I hope not." She put the folder in her briefcase, shut it, then smiled faintly. "They liked the art lessons."

His mouth twisted. "Maybe I should have him take singing next? Country line dancing? Ballet?"

Madge, smiling wryly, shook her head. "It's not a joke, Jed."

"No. I know."

"I didn't have to come back up here until I came to give you the final petition," she told him. "I came because I wanted to give you a chance. I wanted to be able to tell them that you'd got things together." She sighed. "I certainly can't tell them that."

"I told you, it won't happen again!"

Madge shut her briefcase with a snap and stood up. "You have to get your life together, Jed, or you're going to lose that boy. I won't report this. It isn't an official visit. As far as I'm concerned, I didn't even see you today. But I'll be back next week. Wednesday afternoon. And you'd better have some good news for me this time. News that will help me convince them that you're providing a warm, loving home for Tuck."

She picked up her briefcase and went to the door, opened it, then stopped and turned to face him. "And I'm afraid, Jed, that ballet isn't going to do it."

* * *

"I saw Madger goin' down the hill." Tuck dropped his sketch pad on the table and looked at Jed, who was sitting there staring at his coffee mug.

Jed grunted. He shoved away from the table and got more coffee. Madge had made it strong. He needed it strong. He'd never needed it stronger in his life.

"She talked to me," Tuck said.

Jed gave him a sideways glance. The boy had his hands shoved in his pockets with a sort of studied casualness. But if he'd really been casual, Jed knew, he'd have been rummaging through the refrigerator for a snack as he talked.

Now he flicked a gaze in Jed's direction, but the moment their eyes met, he looked away and Jed went back to contemplating the tabletop.

He wished to God he could find some inspiration there, some words that would make the world come right, some reassurance that would set Tuck's mind at ease and convince him that all would be well.

The silence was deafening. Finally Tuck asked, "Do you want me here?"

Jed's head jerked up. "Of course I want you here."

But his adamant declaration was only met by a gaze that was troubled and searching.

"I want you here," Jed said again firmly, flatly. "I'll always want you here."

It was the truth. He only hoped that if Tuck couldn't believe the words, the boy would read it in his face. He held his gaze as steady and unblinking as he could, willing Tuck to see that he meant it.

Finally Tuck's eyes dropped. But the tension in the boy's shoulders eased and a shudder ran through him. He took a breath slowly, deeply, held it a moment, then let it out a bit at a time. "Then we gotta do somethin'. Somethin' that'll make 'em leave us alone."

Jed couldn't argue with that. He also couldn't think of a thing.

Tuck walked over to the window and stared out down the valley. "Somethin' that'll make us look normal."

That didn't sound promising. Or likely. Seconds went by. Minutes passed. Jed willed the alcohol out of his system, prayed for a coherent thought.

"I got it," Tuck said. There was a sudden eager light in his eyes.

"Got what?"

"What we need." Tuck was smiling now. He rocked back on his heels, then bounced on his toes.

The vibration made Jed clench his teeth, but he managed to look hopeful. "What do we need?"

"A wife."

Five

"*A wife!*"

"Uh-huh." Tuck shrugged, but he kept on smiling. "They don't take kids away from two parents. Not unless they're real awful. The parents, I mean, not the kids. So you could hang one on and nobody'd even notice—if you had a wife."

"I'm not going to 'hang one on' again anytime soon!"

"You know what I mean." Tuck brushed him off. Obviously the idea had grabbed him and he was on a roll. "Madger would love it!"

"Madger would." That much of Tuck's farfetched scheme was true. God, what would the kid think of next? "Got someone in mind?" he asked sarcastically.

"Brenna."

Brenna?

Jed's fingers locked on the tabletop. He was glad he was sitting down. Otherwise Tuck's suggestion would have knocked him on his tail.

Tuck wanted him to marry Brenna?

Taking his uncle's stunned silence for an invitation to embellish, Tuck went on. "She could use a husband, too, you know. So her baby'd have a dad. And so she'd have some help runnin' the ranch. Someone better'n Sonny an' Buck. And you gotta admit you know what you're doin'."

He waited for Jed to agree. Jed couldn't say a word.

"It'd be good for her dad, too," Tuck pointed out when no comments were forthcoming. "He could come home if there was somebody who could help him up and down the stairs. An' it'd be really good for me." Another expectant pause.

Jed stared, poleaxed.

Tuck beamed. "I could go to school from Brenna's easier'n from here. Less time on the bus. And of course she'd be there to teach me all I need to know about drawing and painting. And it wouldn't all be one-sided, either, 'cause I could baby-sit if you wanted me to—when the baby comes. I'd learn how," he assured his dazed uncle. "An' Madger'd get off our backs an' everybody'd be happy." Tuck gave the expansive sigh of someone who has solved all the world's problems in one fell swoop. "See?"

Jed saw. Red.

He saw white blinding panic, black despair, deep blue days and a streak of cowardly yellow a mile wide. He didn't move, simply sat bolt upright and stock-still where he was.

"It'd be perfect," Tuck told him in case he hadn't figured it out yet. Then at the continued lack of response, the boy added just a little more hesitantly, "Don'tcha think?"

Jed mustered his brain cells, got them organized. Moved. He shoved his chair back so hard it fell over as he stood up.

"The hell it would," he said hoarsely. And walked out without looking back.

It didn't bear thinking about.
Marrying Brenna.
He wouldn't touch the notion with a ten-foot pole.
Marrying Brenna.
He'd die first.
Marrying Brenna.

It was the last thing he wanted.

Marrying Brenna.

It was all he'd wanted eleven years before.

And then he'd blown it.

Now, as Jed sat astride his horse and stared unseeingly out across the valley, he wished his heart would stop hammering, wished his pulse would stop racing, wished his mind would stop playing with the notion.

He *wasn't* marrying Brenna!

Not then. Not now. Not ever.

If it had once been his dream, it was no longer. It was a dream he'd shattered himself. A dream he had no business even considering again.

So he wasn't.

Couldn't. It just wasn't in the cards.

It didn't make sense.

It didn't!

It did. He shut his eyes. God help him, it did.

Everything Tuck had said was true. Brenna did need help on the ranch. She did need someone who could run things responsibly, someone who didn't get drunk—or at least rarely and only under great provocation. She needed someone to help with her father. She needed someone to be the father of her child.

No.

Jed shoved the thought away. It came right back, nudging its way into the corner of his mind. He turned back to the fence line he was supposed to be checking. It distracted him from that. It poked its way back into his thoughts, diverting him from the view he'd always loved of the valley and the Crazy Mountains.

That sight had always been able to make him forget any problem or put his worst nightmare in perspective. It wasn't touching this one.

"Crazy," he muttered. "That's exactly what it is."

And perfectly logical, too.

People didn't get married for sensible reasons! They didn't get married to keep ranches going and bring fathers home and put off social workers and help each other raise a child! They married for love.

He loved Brenna Jamison.

"No." He said the word aloud and so sharply that his horse whinnied and shied restlessly beneath him, and he had to gather her together and hold her steady. "It's all right," he murmured to soothe her.

But it wasn't all right.

God knew—and Jed knew—it wasn't all right at all.

He stayed away all day, returning to the cabin only when darkness meant risking his horse on rough terrain. He was too good a cowboy to endanger an animal unnecessarily so when night came on, he went back. Tuck had the lights on. He had opened a can of stew and had it simmering on the stove. Jed's stomach growled at the smell. He rubbed it self-consciously and avoided Tuck's gaze.

Tuck, who had apparently decided that more suggestions of who Jed ought to marry might not be in his best interest, barely looked up from the couch where he sat with a book.

"Thanks for puttin' dinner on," Jed said.

Tuck's shoulders moved, but he didn't answer.

Just as well, Jed thought. The less said, the better. He dished up the stew and sat down at the table. Tuck came over and sat opposite him.

They ate. Neither ever talked a lot. Now they didn't talk at all. And the silence held none of the easy camaraderie that they usually shared. In its place a gulf as wide as an ocean lapped between them. Tuck only ventured glances in Jed's direction when he thought Jed wasn't looking. Jed could think of nothing to say to Tuck. They spent the entire evening avoiding each other's eyes.

It wasn't until Tuck was ready for bed that he spoke. Once he had brushed his teeth, he came to the doorway between the bedroom and the main room to stand looking at Jed who pretended to read a stock magazine.

"My ma told me you could be selfish," Tuck said. "I didn't used to believe her."

Then he shut the light off and closed the door on Jed's startled face.

"'Bout time," Otis groused when Brenna arrived at the nursing home on Monday afternoon. "Thought you'd be here Saturday or at least yesterday. Where the hell you been? McCall get the herd shaped up? Things go all right?"

"We missed you, but we managed. The shipping went off on schedule." Brenna bent and kissed her father's dry cheek and wondered why she had thought that today's visit was going to be any easier than the other ones.

Her father did not take easily to his body letting him down. Now he made a harrumphing sound and nodded to the bedside chair. "Sit down and tell me everything."

She knew from experience that when he said "everything" that was precisely what he meant. She had a doctor's appointment back in Livingston at three and she had to go to the tack shop and the hardware store and the grocery store before then, but she knew better than to try to cut things short. She started to talk.

Every two seconds her father stopped her.

What about thus-and-such a steer? he wanted to know. What about this or that one? She wished Jed was there to answer his questions.

"Shoulda brought McCall," her father muttered.

"I'm sure he's quite busy," Brenna said. She had wondered if he would reappear at the ranch sometime during the weekend, but he hadn't. She supposed her fanciful thinking had been just that—fanciful. "He took a lot of time off from Taggart's to help us. And now we don't need him anymore."

Otis harrumphed again. "Shoulda stayed with me 'stead of goin' to the Joneses." He looked at her narrowly. "He tryin' to come back?"

"No," she assured her father. "He was just helping out. So did Taggart and his friend, Noah, and Mace."

"Mighta known young Nichols would stick his nose in."

"He helped a great deal."

Otis plucked fitfully at the blanket and pursed his lips. "Young upstart. That's what he is. Startin' his own herd."

"You did the same thing, Daddy, at his age."

Otis scowled. "More land then. Not the same thing at all." But the look on his face told Brenna he recognized the truth of what she said.

She sympathized with his irritability, aware that it was a result of his desire to be up and doing again, of his frustration with the body that was betraying him. If he were feeling better he'd be cheering the "young upstarts" on.

"Anyhow, now you got the cattle shipped, you can talk to the doctor," Otis said. "Get me out of here."

"I'll talk to him," Brenna promised. But she knew the problem was only partly the rehab he didn't want to do. It was also partly her own inability to help him move around. She was getting awkward enough on her own as the baby grew. Maybe if he would agree to a nurse coming and staying with them . . .

She suggested it.

"Don't need a nurse. Not an invalid. Just want to go home," Otis said now, petulant as a child.

"I know, Daddy." Brenna squeezed his hand. He gave hers a weak press in return.

She stayed with him until he fell asleep. It made her rushed for time, but that was better than leaving before he was ready to let her go.

Still, she didn't have time to grab a bite of lunch. By the time she'd gone to the tack shop and picked up the bridle she'd dropped off last week and then stopped to do the grocery shopping, she had to rush to get to her own doctor's appointment back in Livingston.

Her stomach growled and her baby kicked as she drove. Brenna patted them both. "Later," she promised. She had to park a block from the doctor's office, and when she got out the wind knifed into her back. She tugged her jacket around her and hurried. She was already ten minutes late. Snow clouds were moving in from the Bridgers.

She hoped Dr. Mathis wasn't running as far behind as she was. She had no doubt before long the snow would begin. She wanted to be home before it flew.

Jed saw her as she came out of the building across the street.

He'd come to town to run some errands for Taggart. They were done, but he wasn't heading back. He was just sitting in his truck being haunted by Tuck's words for the five millionth time, telling himself that it wasn't selfishness, it was self-preservation.

He couldn't just drive up to Brenna Jamison's ranch house and ask her to marry him, damn it, no matter how many problems it would solve. If that made him selfish, well, he guessed Tuck was right.

It still stuck in his craw, what the boy had said that night. Hell, what right did Marcy have calling him selfish? She was the one took off and never looked back, leaving him to keep an eye on their ma through her final illness. And wasn't it Marcy who'd come home with a squalling baby and pestered him for help every time he'd had a day off? Not that he'd minded too much once Tuck could toddle and talk. But she had a fine lot of brass calling him selfish just because he kept his own counsel, tried to solve his own problems and went his own way.

Jed scowled and flicked the key in the ignition. He glanced up to see if there was any traffic coming—and there she was, as big as life, on the top step of the building across the street, one hand braced against the wall, one on her distended abdomen.

His teeth came together. His fists clenched. He automatically tugged down his hat so if she happened to look his way, she wouldn't be able to tell who was sitting in the driver's seat of Jed McCall's battered brown pickup truck.

He was groaning at his own foolishness when he saw her start down the steps. She stumbled, caught herself by grabbing the railing, then almost staggered at the bottom, where she still clung to the railing as if it were a life raft in a stormy sea.

Jed was out of the truck and across the street in an instant. "Brenna? What's wrong?"

Her face was as white as a snow-blanketed field. The only color in it seemed to be the bluish-purple hue of her lips. Still she didn't let go of the railing.

Jed reached out and touched her arm. "Are you sick?"

She shook her head, then looked at him little dazed, as if the movement disturbed her equilibrium. "N-no. I'm all right."

Jed's teeth came together with a snap. "Like hell. Here." He took her arm and virtually pried her away from the railing. "Come on. Sit down."

The closest place he could take her to sit was his truck. Any other time he would have balked at the idea. Now he slipped an arm around her and, practically holding her up, hauled her across the street.

"Really, I'm fine," she protested. But once she was sitting, she slumped against the back of the seat and shut her eyes. There was still damn little color in her cheeks.

"Are you gonna faint?"

She shook her head. Slowly she opened her eyes and looked at him. "No."

He breathed a sigh of relief. "What happened?"

She smiled faintly. "I missed lunch."

He stared.

She shrugged. "That's all. Really. I'm not usually such a hothouse plant. It's just...being pregnant. You remember when we were out on the range, how I need to stop and eat?"

He remembered. God, did he!

"The baby doesn't like missing meals. My body doesn't like me missing meals. It's stupid, but there it is."

"It's not stupid," Jed said, suddenly furious that, along with everything else she had to worry about, she wasn't even getting proper nutrition. Without another word he stalked around the truck, got in and started the engine. He shoved it in reverse and backed out of the parking space.

Brenna sat up straight. "What are you doing?"

"Feeding you lunch."

There was a diner two blocks away. By himself he would have walked. He was pretty certain Brenna wouldn't make that. He parked right out front, hopped out and went around, opening the door for her and taking her arm to help her get down.

"I'm all right," she told him, but she didn't pull her arm out of his grasp. In fact, she seemed quite willing to lean into him just a bit as they walked the few steps to the restaurant and went in. He held her tighter.

"Ah, Jed, 'bout time you paid us a visit." Kacy, the teenage waitress who always flirted with him, beamed. But her eyes widened slightly when she saw who he was bringing with him. "Ms. Jamison."

Jed steered Brenna into a booth, helped her off with her jacket and hung it on the hook beside the seat. Then he hung his own jacket up and slid in across from her. "Bring her a cup of hot tea," he told Kacy. "Now. I'll have coffee."

Fortunately Kacy was quick. As soon as she reappeared, Jed tipped the tall glass sugar container over Brenna's tea, then stirred it and pushed it in front of her. "Drink."

She made a face. "I don't like sugar in tea."

"Tough." He leveled his gaze on her. "You need it."

She sighed, but then she clasped the mug in both hands and raised it to her lips. Steam curled around her face as she sipped, then made another face.

"Drink," Jed insisted. "More."

Brenna took another sip and then another. There was just a hint of color coming back. Kacy returned with Jed's coffee. "Thanks. What's the special?"

"Roast beef sandwiches, mashed potatoes and gravy. Cole slaw or three bean salad."

"Bring us each one. Cole slaw."

"I don't—" Brenna began, but Kacy, bless her infatuated heart, wasn't paying any attention to Brenna. She just nodded at Jed's orders and scurried toward the kitchen. When he turned back to Brenna again, he was relieved to see even more color in her cheeks.

"Better?" he asked.

She set the mug down, but kept her hands wrapped around it. "Yes. Thank you." She shot him a quick, almost shy, glance, then looked down again. "You've gone to a lot of trouble for me...us—" she corrected quickly "—these last few days."

"No trouble." He took a swallow of coffee. It wasn't very hot, but it was strong and black, and the mug gave him something to hang on to now that the reality of sitting across the table from Brenna was beginning to set in.

Had he lost his mind?

"How come you didn't eat?" he asked her after a moment. "I mean, if you know it's gonna bother you..."

"No time. I went to Bozeman to see my dad and to do some errands. I stayed with him longer than I'd intended. He isn't easy to...abandon. And then I had to hurry back here for a doctor's appointment and—"

"You are sick!"

"No. It's perfectly routine. For the baby. I'm supposed to go every three weeks." She flushed slightly and looked away, as if talking about her pregnancy with him made her uncomfortable.

It made him uncomfortable, too, but he couldn't seem to leave it alone. He shredded his napkin. "How, um, how far along are you?"

"Seven months. I'm due in December."

Kacy came back bringing them cole slaw and plates of roast beef and mashed potatoes, swimming in dark brown gravy. She poured Jed more coffee and offered Brenna more hot water.

Brenna smiled and thanked her. She stirred her tea. Jed picked up his fork. "Eat up."

Brenna took a bite, then shut her eyes and something that sounded almost like a whimper came from deep in her throat.

Jed looked at her, alarmed. "What's the matter?"

Her eyes flicked open. She smiled. "Nothing. It just—" her throat worked, she swallowed "—tastes so good."

The look on her face was so blissful it made him laugh. "Good. There's more where that came from if you're still hungry."

They ate the rest of the meal without speaking. Jed cleaned his own plate quickly and leaned back, replete, and allowed himself the luxury of watching her. Just for a few minutes, he told himself. What could a few minutes hurt?

She didn't look at him, which made it easier. She concentrated entirely on the food on her plate until there was almost nothing left except one of the soggy crusts of bread and a little cabbage in the bottom of the cole slaw bowl.

Only then did she shove her plate back and look up to find his eyes on her. "You must think I'm a pig."

Jed shook his head. *Okay, buster, your few minutes are up,* he told himself. He ought to be looking away right about now. Sitting here staring at Brenna Jamison was plumb foolish. It made the heat start to curl open and spread inside him. It made his body hard and his mind soft.

It made him remember Tuck's suggestion. He set his cup down with a bang.

Kacy came running with the pot. "Sorry," she gabbled. "I wasn't payin' enough attention."

Jed reddened. "Don't matter," he said to Kacy, but he let her fill his cup, anyway.

"You want some more hot water, Ms. Jamison?" Kacy asked her. "And another tea bag?"

"No," Jed started to say, eager suddenly to be on his way. He'd daydreamed long enough.

But Brenna said, "Thank you. That would be lovely." Then she looked at Jed. "Sorry. Did you want to leave?"

He shook his head. "Take your time." He slumped back in his seat. The napkin was in a million bits. He looked around for something else to shred. Brenna was smiling at him again.

"I owe you one," she said.

He shrugged uncomfortably. "At least you got some color in your cheeks now."

She touched one self-consciously. "Probably from the wind."

"From a square meal."

"Thanks to you."

"I couldn't let you fall over on the curb."

"There was a time when I thought you might have done just that," she said.

There it was again, the hurt. The question. The accusation. He sat up straight and took a death lock on the coffee cup. "I would never—" He stopped.

She met his gaze, waited.

He couldn't finish. He just shook his head resolutely.

"You would never..." Her voice trailed off. Her gaze didn't. It met his, square and unwavering.

He looked away, swore under his breath, then ran his tongue over his lips. "That's past," he said hoarsely.

Kacy brought the tea bag and more hot water. Brenna thanked her, ripped the bag out of its cover and put it in the cup, then poured the hot water over it. She did it all with careful deliberation. At last, when the tea bag was finished steeping, she looked up again. It seemed to him that the color in her cheeks had faded some.

"So it is," she said quietly. "So it is."

What hurt was that he was so damn *nice*.

He acted like he cared. He rescued her on the street, saved her from making a fool of herself in front of the pedestrians of downtown Livingston. He got her hot, sweet tea and saw that she got a cowboy-sized lunch. He even followed her all the way home. He did everything to make those fanciful thoughts come back.

And then he said, "It's past."

Well, all right, damn it. It *was* past.

So she tried to pretend she didn't see his truck in the rearview mirror all the way home. She tried not to notice that he followed her all the way to the yard. Thank God he didn't get out. She didn't think she could invite him in, play the genial, polite hostess.

"It's past," she told herself again. "Get used to it."

He would be a casual acquaintance. A neighbor.

Still, she was glad he didn't get out of his truck. She took a grocery sack out of the back and started slowly and awkwardly up the steps. She tried to be as graceful as possible so he wouldn't think she was going to stumble again.

There were three more sacks, but she left them, afraid that he might come and help her. She was grateful, but she'd had enough neighborliness for one day. So she turned on the porch and gave him a quick smile and a wave.

"Goodbye! Thank you again!"

Then she turned and went briskly into the house. She shut the door and leaned against it, not moving until she heard his truck drive away. Then she breathed again. Then she went back for the other groceries. Then she made herself another cup of tea.

With milk this time, not sugar. She hated sugar in tea but knew, under the circumstances, that Jed had been right. Then she'd needed energy.

Now she needed calm.

She took her tea into the living room and started a fire in the fireplace. Then she picked up the new magazine she'd bought and settled in front of the blaze.

Calm, she told herself, tipping her head back against the sofa, breathing deeply. Calm. She took a sip of tea.

The knock on the back door was so sudden and unexpected, that she spilled tea down the front of her sweater.

"Damn." She mopped at it as the knock came again, this one more impatient than the first. She hurried to answer it.

Jed stood on the porch, white-faced. "How 'bout we get married?"

Six

"It was Tuck's idea," he went on, aware that he'd blown it.

But, hell and damnation, it wasn't like he'd ever proposed before! He wouldn't be proposing now if he had the sense God gave a goat.

Trouble was, he'd sat in his truck and watched her get out of her car. He'd seen the way she'd struggled with that grocery bag. He hadn't a doubt in the world she had more groceries to be unloaded, but he hadn't asked. He hadn't rolled down the window and said a word. Because he hadn't wanted to know.

He'd only wanted to run.

He'd seen her struggle, had seen her smile gamely and wave. She hadn't wanted him there any more than he wanted to be there.

So what in God's name was he doing back?

And proposing marriage, of all things?

He needed his head examined. And his heart.

Because that was the problem. Much as he wanted to run, he couldn't. Once before he'd left Brenna Jamison—because he wasn't any good for her.

Now he was back and proposing marriage because—whether she wanted to or not, whether *he* wanted it or not—in one way, at least, she did need a man like him.

Her tasks were too big for her alone. He knew she wouldn't complain about them. He knew she'd never ask for help. She'd struggle and fight on as long as she was able.

But she would never be able to bring her father home and she knew it. She'd be lucky if she could cope with her coming child. How she would winter on the ranch—just her and the child—didn't bear thinking about.

It was about that time that he swore fiercely and turned the truck around.

He was doing it for Tuck, he told himself. For Madger the Badger and her whole damned bureaucratic bunch of snoops. He was doing it for Brenna. For her father. For the future of the ranch. For her child.

And this time he *wouldn't* fail—not any of them.

And himself?

No. He wouldn't let himself think about that.

"Tuck thinks we should get married?" Brenna stared at him, her eyes dark and unreadable. Her tone sounded almost conversational, but he saw that her knuckles were white.

"'S what he said. Got it all figured out, Tuck does." Jed tried to sound as nonchalant as she did. "He said it would solve everybody's problems. I reckon he's right."

"You do." It wasn't a question. It was skeptical.

Jed felt the heat rise above the collar of his jacket. He shifted from one boot to the other. "Could I, um, maybe come in?" He didn't know if it would be easier, but it couldn't be much worse.

Wordlessly Brenna stepped back to let him pass. He went into the kitchen, leaned his hip pockets against the counter, took off his hat and tried to put into words, as well as Tuck had, all the reasons they ought to do it. Jed didn't seem to have the same verbal gifts.

He mumbled about him being able to take care of the ranch while she took care of the baby. He chuntered on about being able to help her father when they brought him home, and about her being able to give Tuck art lessons, and eventually he got around to Madger and the petition. He didn't want to mention that, but he figured he owed her a straight story.

"You'd be doin' us a favor, too," he said, explaining about her visit, omitting the part about the whiskey bottle and the hangover. There were some things he figured she didn't need to know. "Anyhow, it'd get Madger—Madge Bowen—off our backs, Tuck says. An' I reckon he's right about that, too."

"Tuck's a regular oracle," Brenna said dryly.

"A what?"

"Never mind. Is Madge Bowen really threatening to take Tuck away from you?" There was an edge to Brenna's voice he'd never heard before.

He flicked a glance at her, then contemplated his fingers creasing his hat brim. "She doesn't want to. If it was up to her, she'd probably leave well enough alone, figurin' I might not be the best there is, but I'm kin and I try. But you know these agencies. They get their teeth in somethin' and they just rag it to death. Right now—" he lifted his shoulders "—what they're raggin' is me."

"They're crazy! You're a fine guardian."

Jed's head jerked up at her vehemence. He looked at her, amazed. "Well, that's kinda what I thought, too. But I haven't ever been good at convincin' people like Madger. Not with words anyhow."

"So you thought you'd marry me instead?" There was something new in her tone, a hint of amusement? He wasn't sure.

He shrugged awkwardly. "Like my ma used to say, 'You scratch my back, I'll scratch yours.'"

"Would you scratch my back if we were married, Jed?"

"What?"

The soft challenge of her words sent a jolt of panic straight through him. He flushed to the roots of his hair. He opened his mouth to speak, but nothing would come out.

"I—" he stammered finally, cleared his throat, tried again. "I didn't think—I mean, that's not what I—"

"Not what you meant?"

"No!" Still scarlet, he tried to muster just a little coherence. "I...would...scratch your back...if you wanted me to," he managed at last, not even able to look at her when he said the words. He'd have to buy a new hat. He'd crushed this one beyond all recognition.

"Thank you," she said almost formally.

Hell. But then what had he expected? That she'd throw her arms around him and pledge undying love? After what he'd done to her? He pressed the heel of one boot into the toe of the other.

"Forget it," he muttered, turning toward the door. He already had his hand on the knob when her voice stopped him.

"Wait."

Jed waited, but he didn't turn. He didn't want to look at her. He didn't want to see in her eyes what a presumptuous idiot he'd been.

"I'll marry you," she said.

She couldn't even put it down to light-headedness from missing lunch. She was stuffed—still—six hours later.

And engaged, apparently.

To Jed McCall.

"Be careful what you pray for," she muttered as she slipped into bed and lay in the darkness, staring up at the moonlit ceiling. It was beginning to sound like a litany.

Engaged to Jed McCall.

It was almost funny. It would be if somewhere deep inside she didn't still hurt. What had he been thinking of, proposing to her like that?

What had *she* been thinking of, accepting?

Well, he'd spelled the answer out, really. Advantages for all of them: Tuck, her child, her father, her ranch, her.

She couldn't exactly see any advantages to Jed at the moment. But maybe she wasn't looking at it from his point of view. She turned on her side and shoved a pillow up against her abdomen to support it and the child.

When she was eighteen she had pretended that pillow was Jed. She'd rubbed her cheek against its percale softness and hugged it tight against her and whispered love words to it and lived for the day when she would do the same to Jed.

The day had never come.

Would it now? Would he share her bed in this . . . this business arrangement they'd agreed to?

Clearly he still had some reaction to her. If he hadn't, he would have maintained a complete stone face when she'd made that flippant remark about his scratching her back.

He'd blushed. She couldn't remember the last time she'd seen Jed McCall blush.

Well, actually she could—but she didn't want to remember it. Not tonight. Tonight was far too fraught with emotion already.

The baby kicked inside her, and she shifted slightly, adjusting the pillow.

"Will you kick Jed?" she asked it, then smiled. "Sometimes I'd like to kick Jed."

She snuggled down against the pillow and wrapped her arms tighter around it. She would sleep, she decided, and in the morning it would be better. Doubtless she would wake up and find that she'd imagined the whole thing. The day's idiocies would be nothing more than the aberrant mental wandering of an overstressed, very weary almost-mother. A dream within a dream.

And if it was real? If tomorrow Jed came back and said he wasn't kidding? If tomorrow, when she woke up, she was still engaged to marry Jed McCall?

She was afraid to think about that.

The notion of marrying Brenna Jamison was scary enough. What happened after word got out didn't bear thinking about.

He should have kept his fool mouth shut. He should have damned well spirited her off to Reno or Vegas or one of those places where you got married and told everybody about it afterward.

He made the mistake of telling Tuck.

Tuck told Becky. Becky told Susannah. Susannah told Tess. Tess told Felicity. Felicity told Jenny. Jenny told Mace. Or maybe Taggart told Mace. Or Mace told Taggart.

Jed had lost the thread of gossip leading to his downfall pretty quick. It didn't matter. Before twenty-four hours were up the whole damned valley knew.

And though Brenna agreed to go with him to see Dan Morgan, the justice of the peace, a week from Friday afternoon, no one else thought that was any place to get married.

"You're going to get married in some office?" Felicity said when she finally got him to admit he and Brenna were in fact tying the knot. "Don't be ridiculous!"

"It's not ridiculous," Jed said. He was backing toward the door and wishing he'd never set foot in Felicity's kitchen.

"You can't get married in an office!" Tess said flatly. She was sitting at the table doing absolutely nothing. It looked to Jed as if Felicity had simply called her to come over and be reinforcements. "If you don't want to do it at church, at least do it at the ranch."

"It'd be too much work for Brenna," he said, almost to the door. Another two feet and he'd be free.

"Not a bit of it," Felicity said. She and Tess and Felicity and Jenny would take care of everything.

"But—"

"Everything," Tess said firmly. She got up and came toward him. He angled away. It put him farther from the door but also farther from Tess. "What kind of flowers does she like? Chocolate cake? We had a chocolate-and-white with almond filling. Think she'd like that?"

Jed shook his head helplessly. "We don't need—"

"You do," they told him in no uncertain terms.

And in case he doubted it, they surrounded him the following day in the barn and backed him up against the horse stall and told him it was all settled.

"Daisies," Tess said. "She likes daisies."

"And chocolate-and-white cake will be fine," Felicity said.

"We talked to Brenna," Jenny told him in case he hadn't already figured that out.

"And Judge Morgan," said Tess.

Jed gaped.

"You can get married at the ranch," she went on.

"A week from Saturday morning," said Jenny.

"Eleven o'clock." That was Felicity.

"Reception after." Tess.

"What?"

"Don't worry. I told you, we'll take care of everything." Felicity patted his cheek. "All you have to do is show up."

Then, leaving him standing dumbstruck, they turned as one and headed toward the door.

There Felicity had an afterthought. She turned back to Jed again. "Dress for the occasion."

And Jenny advised, "A clean pair of jeans won't do."

"Buy a suit," Tess counseled.

Then they left, leaving Jed reeling in their wake.

Taggart and Noah, deputized by their wives, took him in hand. Three days later they dragged him off to Bozeman to buy a suit.

"A suit? Where the hell else am I ever gonna wear a suit?"

"We can bury you in it," Taggart suggested, and the look he gave Jed said plainly enough that they'd be doing just that if he gave them any more trouble.

Jed bought the suit. He bought a long-sleeved white shirt. He bought a tie. A subdued burgundy-and-charcoal stripe, one hundred percent silk. It might as well have been hemp, the way it felt like a noose around his neck.

The suit made him feel like an impostor.

"So what else is new?" he asked himself grimly the morning of his wedding, when he finally mustered up the guts to put it on and stare at himself in the mirror.

Tuck, hovering in the doorway to the bedroom observing his uncle, raised his brows. "Weird," he said.

You can say that again, Jed thought.

He wanted to bolt. To ride off into the sunset and never look back. Instead, in less than three hours he was going to be marrying Brenna Jamison. The love of his life. The woman he wanted more than any woman in the world.

A woman who—regardless of whether they were married or not—he was afraid to touch.

The phone rang. "It's Brenna," Tuck said.

Jed's stomach lurched. Was she crying off? His emotions roller-coastered.

He grabbed the receiver with a clammy hand. "What?"

"Hi." Her voice sounded as shaky as his. Oddly, that helped.

He'd hardly seen her since his proposal. It had seemed smarter to stay away. Less chance of making an ass of himself. "What's up?"

"Tess said you're wearing a suit." She sounded miserable.

He frowned, looking down at the navy pinstripe wool, wondering how she could tell and if she thought he looked like an impostor, too. "Taggart and Noah made me."

"Can you take it back?"

"Take it back? You mean you don't want—" He stopped, suddenly hollow.

"I . . . don't have a dress. Not a . . . formal dress. For a wedding, I mean."

That was the problem? "You mean you still want—"

"Were you hoping I'd called to say it was all off?"

"No," he said quickly. Then, "No," in a more moderate tone.

"I probably should, but . . . I do need . . . it's just . . . I'd feel funny if you were in a suit and I . . ." She sounded fragile, at the end of her rope. The way he felt.

"I can take it back," Jed said firmly. He was unknotting the tie even as he spoke. He yanked it out from beneath the collar buttons and tossed it on the bed, then shrugged out of the coat. One-handed he began to undo the buttons on the shirt.

Tuck watched from the doorway, eyes like silver dollars. "Aren'tcha marryin' her, then?"

Jed ignored him. "I got a clean pair of jeans. Are they okay?" he asked Brenna as he slipped out of the shirt, then unbuckled his belt.

"Wonderful." She was definitely breathing easier, though there was still a catch in her voice.

He dropped his trousers.

"Jed?" she said.

"Hmm?"

"I was just wondering, I know what I'm getting out of this marriage. And what my father is getting. And Tuck. And the baby. But...what about you?"

"Me?"

"What are you getting?"

Temptation, Jed thought. Pain. Anguish. Frustration. *The only woman I'll ever love.*

"The joy of not having to get married in a suit," he said. "I'll see you in a couple of hours."

She was marrying Jed McCall.

She was marrying Jed McCall? Apparently she was. In three hours. Two hours. One hour. Forty minutes. Twenty.

"He's here," Becky reported from her post by the bedroom window.

"So's Tuck," said Susannah. "Look. His hair is combed!"

"So's Jed's," said Becky, awestruck.

"How can you tell?" Susannah asked. "He's wearin' his hat."

"A *hat!*" This last was from Susannah's mother, Tess. She left off pinning Brenna's hair up and flew to the window to peer out, Felicity and Jenny close on her heels. "He *is!*" she affirmed, aghast.

"And jeans!" Jenny was horrified. "I thought he—"

"I told him to," Brenna said quickly. She didn't follow them to the window. She didn't want to look. Didn't want to see. Not now. Not yet.

All three women and both little girls turned on her. Tess, Jenny and Felicity looked astonished. So did Susannah. Only Becky nodded as if she understood.

Probably she did. Brenna sensed a kindred spirit in Taggart's daughter. Even though Becky was wearing a dress today, it was the first Brenna had ever seen her in.

"I didn't want him wearing a suit, because I don't have a wedding dress."

"But we would've got you one!" Tess protested.

"I know, but I didn't want you to. It wouldn't...feel right."

And not just for the reason she gave them, either. For all that she had loved Jed for years—still did love him—she couldn't bring herself to stand up with Jed in formal attire.

Once she had dreamed of doing just that. Once she *would* have done just that, if things had happened the way she'd hoped. They hadn't. To do so now seemed to make a mockery of what was real and honest about those dreams. Her marriage to Neil had felt more real, more honest than this one.

But she couldn't say that to Tess and Felicity and Jenny. They might have some notion that things were a little rushed and awkward, but they were romantic enough to believe that there was real love between her and Jed.

She couldn't disillusion them, she told herself.

Or—the question was as prompt as it was unwelcome—was she afraid of disillusioning herself?

"It's your wedding," Tess said. "Have it the way you want." She smiled. "Have Jed the way you want him, too." She waggled her eyebrows.

Brenna blushed. She couldn't help it. Felicity and Tess laughed at her.

Jenny, long married, shook her head. "Come on. Let's finish your hair and get on with it. In a few hours it won't matter. You won't be wearing anything at all!"

The little girls gaped, then giggled and looked out the window, studying Jed and tittering at the same time.

Were they wondering what he'd look like when he wasn't "wearing anything at all"? Brenna wondered. She was. She hadn't seen "all" of Jed since he was fifteen and had caught him skinny-dipping. He'd been little more than a boy then.

Later, well, she had wished. Dreamed. Hoped. But she had wanted to wait until they were married. Jed had, too. Or at least he'd been willing. Or she'd thought he had. Until Cheree.

She shoved the thought away. She wasn't going to think about Cheree now!

She focused on Jed again. Would she see all of him now, in a few short hours?

Would theirs be that kind of marriage?

Of course it would. This wasn't the eighteenth century, for heaven's sake! And even back then a marriage of convenience also brought with it the convenience of sex. How could she think otherwise?

Well, she didn't. She just hadn't let herself think about it until now.

As she did, she pressed her hands against her burgeoning belly and realized that the sword cut both ways. He would be seeing her naked, too.

Dear God, no! She couldn't appear before him like this!

"Baby kicking?" Tess sympathized with a smile.

In fact the baby wasn't moving. It was obviously hiding out. Brenna wished she could hide out, too. "It's fine," she said, managing a faint smile.

"Here's Judge Morgan now," Becky announced. "They're comin' in!"

Tess ran the brush through Brenna's hair one last time, pronounced her a beautiful bride, then squeezed her hands. "All set?"

Brenna swallowed, took an unsteady breath, then nodded.

"Good," Tess said. "It's time."

He'd thought asking her was the hard part.

Not so. The minute Jed looked up from where he stood in front of the fireplace to see Brenna coming down the stairs toward him, he began to understand that the hard part hadn't even begun.

How in the world was he going to live day after day, month after month with a woman who could set him on fire with a mere look, and keep their marriage the business arrangement he'd proposed?

Yet if he gave in ... if he dared ...

Jed's fingers locked into fists. The fire, which moments ago had only seemed the source of a pleasant warmth, now threatened to consume him. He ran a dry tongue over even drier lips and watched as Brenna reached the bottom of the stairs.

She was wearing a simple hunter green maternity dress, its soft wool draping her fullness gently, making her look more lovely than a traditional wedding dress would have—at least in his eyes.

He was grateful he wasn't wearing that silk noose of a tie. His emotions alone threatened to choke him. His breath came in shallow unsteady gulps.

Three times during the course of the few minutes during which they listened to Judge Morgan and exchanged their vows, Jed caught Brenna looking worriedly at him. Did she think he was going to faint?

Was he?

He swallowed audibly and dragged in another desperate lungful of air.

"Do you, Jed, take this woman, Brenna . . ." Judge Morgan began, and there it was—the stuff of his dreams. And nightmares.

Jed stared at the floor after the judge had finished speaking, afraid he'd blurt the words too soon, afraid of making a fool of himself by appearing too eager.

Was he eager? He hadn't thought so. Once maybe.

But now? He considered that.

Taggart cleared his throat. Jed jerked his gaze up. Judge Morgan was looking at him expectantly. Brenna was looking at him nervously. Tuck kicked his foot impatiently.

"Ido," Jed said, as if it was all one word.

Behind him he heard a couple of girlish giggles. His face felt hotter than the fire that flickered behind the judge, who was now saying something else.

Tuck kicked him again and thrust something at him. The ring. God, yes, the ring. Good thing Tuck had remembered. Jed hadn't. Not once.

He fumbled with it now, then turned and started to look for Brenna's hand.

He found her eyes instead. They were warm as they met his, warm and welcoming and a little worried all at the same time.

Ah, Brenna. He wanted to protect and reassure her. He managed a smile.

She did, too, and he felt her fingers slide into his. Ducking his head, he concentrated on slipping the ring onto her finger.

It was his mother's ring. He figured maybe Brenna would want to pick one of her own after they were married. Or maybe she would want to keep her first ring. From her sculptor, the father of her child.

That at least had been a real marriage. He felt vaguely hollow just thinking about it. He didn't hear what the judge said this time, either.

Tuck groaned audibly and kicked him. Hard.

"Kiss her," he hissed.

Jed's whole body jerked. *Kiss her?*

Why hadn't he remembered that? He looked up to find Brenna's gaze on him once more. Her lips were slightly parted. Her cheeks were flushed. *Kiss her.*

He remembered the first time he'd kissed her, out behind the barn. She'd been seventeen, eager and laughing. She'd teased him for years, but that had been the teasing of a child. The year she was a senior in high school things had changed.

Or maybe *they* changed. Whichever it was, Jed hadn't seen her as a kid anymore, and her teasing had tempted him in ways he'd never before been tempted. When they'd met behind the barn and she'd tickled his cheek with a piece of straw, then danced away from him, he'd grabbed her and found a woman in his arms, not a child. The world had seemed to shift on its axis. He remembered staring down at her, stunned. And then her body had slid against his, her curves had pressed into his angles. And she'd tipped her face up to his, looking at him with such a mixture of hope and longing, that he hadn't been able to resist her.

He couldn't resist her now. This was no place for resistance, anyway, he reminded himself.

She was his wife.

His *wife.*

Jed drew a breath and slid his arms around her, pulling her close. Then he bent his head and kissed her.

He meant it to be a duty peck. A seal to a business deal, which after all was what they had. He meant it to be a sign of his commitment to the bargain they'd struck between them. Just that and nothing more.

He should have known better. The minute his mouth touched hers, he was lost. In the sweet touch of her lips. In the gentle warmth of her embrace. In the soft flutter of her eyelashes against his cheek. For the first time in eleven years he had Brenna in his arms. He didn't want to let go.

He didn't, either, until the repeated clearing of Judge Morgan's throat, the rising crescendo of girlish giggles behind him and another of Tuck's well-placed kicks brought him back to propriety.

He dragged his mouth away from Brenna's and stared down at her, his heart pounding, his chest heaving, his brain reeling, his loins afire.

She stared back at him, her expression equally shocked.

Of course. She would be. She would never expect . . .

Jed's jaw clenched. They just stood—and stared at each other—until at last Tess and Felicity clapped their hands, applauding, breaking the spell.

"Congratulations," Taggart said and clapped him on the back. Mace did the same. And Noah. Their wives all crowded around Brenna.

"Is it over? Are you married?" Tuck demanded.

"Yes," Judge Morgan told him.

Tuck breathed a sigh of relief, then looked at his uncle. "You're not very good at this, are you?"

Jed barely glanced at him. His gaze was still on Brenna. They had stepped apart, but their fingers were still entwined. He wanted to hang on forever.

The temptation was incredible. He knew he didn't dare. Carefully he loosened his fingers and eased them out of her grasp. Hers fell to her sides.

In the babble and jostle of the room where they had been joined, now they were alone.

"Sorry," Jed said as lightly as he could manage and only loud enough for her to hear. "For the kiss, I mean." His heart was still thundering. He could see the pulse hammer in her throat. "I didn't mean . . ." He cleared his throat and lied desperately. "I never meant—" He managed a rueful smile. "That wasn't what I had in mind."

It was, unfortunately, what everyone else had in mind.

"We didn't know what to get you," Felicity told Brenna and Jed over the wedding cake and punch she and Taggart had provided. "It's not like you're setting up housekeeping. We looked around and thought you had almost everything you needed." She beamed. "Except time."

"Together," Jenny added.

"Alone," Tess put in with a smile.

Taggart and Mace and Noah grinned at him. Jed looked confused.

"So we got you a honeymoon," Felicity said.

Noah did his version of a wolf whistle. Taggart managed a credible howl. Mace winked at Jed.

Jed stared at them all, aghast.

"A honeymoon?" Brenna said faintly. She sat down.

"In Cody," Tess explained. "We got you a room for the weekend."

"We're keeping Tuck," Felicity said. "So don't worry about him."

"And I called Brenna's doctor, and he said you just got in under the wire, but it was fine. Just be circumspect." Jenny grinned.

"She means," Mace translated with grin, "have a good time, don't wear out your bride."

Jed's face flamed.

"Mace!" Jenny put her hand over her husband's mouth.

"That's why we decided on Cody," Felicity said. "That way you can go to the museums and look at paintings the...the rest of the time." She tried to sound matter-of-fact, but her face was a little pink, too.

"Though why you'd waste your time on them—" Jenny grinned "—when you can look at Jed naked . . ."

The women all giggled.

Now it was Mace's turn to clamp his hand over her mouth. Susannah and Becky looked him up and down with such frankness he thought he'd die.

Tuck just rolled his eyes. ''Oh, brother.''

Brenna looked away, flustered. Her eye caught Jed's.

He wished that riding off into the sunset was still an option. He wanted to sink through the floor.

A business deal with a ranch, a kid and several hundred head of cattle was something Jed thought he could handle. But a honeymoon in a hotel room in Cody?

He figured there was some truth after all to that business about the vengeance of the Lord. He reckoned he was just about to experience it firsthand.

Seven

He hadn't said a word for a hundred miles. Or more.

Not since they'd turned off the interstate at Laurel and started south. Then he'd said, "Looks like snow."

He was right. It had started snowing a few minutes later. It was still snowing now. Not just a little. A lot. More than New York saw in most winters.

Jed didn't suggest that they stop.

Stop where? Brenna wondered. The towns between Laurel and Cody were not exactly urban metropolises. Three bars, a grocery, a hardware store and a welding shop pretty much summed them up. Nice places to live, but you wouldn't want to visit there. You *couldn't* visit there, not unless you slept in your truck.

So on they went toward Cody. In silence.

It was so quiet—and so white—it seemed they were cocooned in their own little universe. Once, Brenna remembered, she would have given her right arm for a universe with just her and Jed. Once she'd thought Jed would have, too.

Not the man sitting next to her. He was a stranger.

And her husband.

She'd tried making small talk. She'd exhausted that before they left the interstate. He gave her no help at all, the few words he managed only monosyllables. Jed had never been talkative. But today you could get him mixed up with a cigar store Indian.

She talked valiantly about the wedding, about how nice it had been for Tess and Felicity and Jenny to want to make it an occasion to remember. She mentioned the daisies, raved about the cake, said how much she appreciated Noah and Taggart taking Jed to buy a suit, even though she'd asked him not to wear it.

She got grunts, occasional nods, a few stiff words. Hardly worth the effort. Finally Brenna gave up. She was too tired to try anymore. What difference would it make if she did?

She shifted, making herself stare straight ahead, not at Jed. The seat belt pulled against her abdomen. The baby kicked. She pressed her hand against her belly. Out of the corner of her eye, she saw Jed's fingers tighten on the steering wheel.

"You aren't gonna have it *now,* are you?"

She felt a stab of satisfaction that at least something could make him talk. "No." A pause. "I don't think so."

The look he shot her was panic-stricken.

"I promise I won't."

Another longer look seemed to convince him she meant it. "Thank God for that." He sighed and kneaded the back of his neck as if trying to work out some of the tension.

"Would you like me to drive for a while?"

"No." And that was that.

More miles passed. "Blame fool idea sendin' us to Cody," Jed said at last. The snow had let up a bit, but there wasn't much to see beyond the whiteness.

"They thought they were being kind."

He snorted. "Hardly."

If Brenna had dared harbor any hopes that he might in the last few days have come to want her the way he had once wanted her, they were gone in a flash. She folded her hands in her lap and took a deep, careful breath, then let it out again slowly. Something behind her eyes was stinging. Not tears? Please God, not tears. Not after all this time. Not when she'd promised herself she didn't have any illusions left. She held herself absolutely still, willing her body to fight her emotions.

She heard Jed sigh.

"I didn't mean it like that," he said. "It's just...I wasn't bargainin' for any damn honeymoon."

"Do you think I was?"

"No. Of course not." His mouth pressed together in a thin line.

Brenna plucked at the hem of her sweater. "Once we would have." She said the words quietly, probably shouldn't have said them at all.

She heard Jed swallow. His jaw tightened. "Once," he said raggedly. That was all.

They got to Cody late that evening. In time for bed.

The last thing Jed wanted under the circumstances. He wondered if he dared ask for a room with two doubles. But before he could muster up the courage, the motel clerk said, "Hi, Jed."

It was Jenny's kid sister, Teresa. He didn't remember where she'd moved when she married and left Elmer. Now he knew.

She beamed at them. "I made sure you got the bridal suite." Swell.

"I had a crush on him once," she confided to a wide-eyed Brenna. "He didn't know I was alive."

Jed, mortified, couldn't even glance in Brenna's direction. He practically snatched the key from Teresa's hand. "Which room?"

Teresa laughed. "Eager, aren't you? Room 27. Down the hall, up the stairs. Far end. Where no one will bother you," she added with a giggle. Then her gaze dropped to Brenna's protruding abdomen. "I guess you've found places like that before." She reddened slightly. "Jenny didn't tell me that. Want some help with your bags?"

"No." Jed practically shoved Brenna down the hall, feeling Teresa's speculative gaze on them all the way. Couldn't Brenna move a little faster?

It wasn't until they got into the room and he shut the door behind them that he got a good look at her pale face and trembling hands and he realized how exhausted she was. He muttered under his breath, dropped their bags and helped her off with her coat.

"Are you all right?"

"Yes." But she was shivering and pale, hugging herself in the dim light of the room.

"You look like hell."

"Thank you very much."

"You hungry?" He remembered the time he'd found her in Livingston when she'd almost fallen down the steps. "You didn't eat much at the—" He hesitated over the word, then said it. "The reception. Want me to get you something to eat? I'm pretty sure this place doesn't have room service, but I can go out and bring something back."

She sank down into the sofa beneath the window and looked up at him, her face still ghostly looking. "That would be wonderful. Anything you want."

He wanted to get out of here. He'd stopped focusing entirely on Brenna's washed-out face and was now capable of taking in the larger picture—including the bed.

It was big and inviting, plumped with a feather tick and full of lacy romantic-looking pillows and such. He headed toward the door. "You should've said. We could have stopped and eaten along the way."

"Oh? Where?" A faint grin touched her mouth.

He rubbed a hand against the back of his neck and grimaced wryly, then scowled at the bed again. "We could've gone back."

"They all would have been so disappointed."

The hell with them, Jed wanted to say. *Do they have any idea what they're doing to me?*

No, of course they didn't. And neither did Brenna, sitting there all pale and fragile and delectable as hell.

"I'll be back," he said.

He wished to God it didn't have to be anytime soon.

He brought back barbecued beef sandwiches, cole slaw and cups of coffee. He remembered she liked milk, no sugar, in hers, so even though he thought the sugar might give her energy, he put in milk.

Brenna looked at it, then at him. She smiled.

He smiled back and spread the food out on napkins in the middle of the coffee table in front of the sofa. The coffee table was small and they were in danger of knocking things off. But the only alternative was the bed.

Jed refused to look at that.

Brenna must have showered while he was gone, for her loose hair was damp at the ends, and her cheeks, though still pale, had a freshly scrubbed look. It reminded him of the time he'd gone to see her when she'd broken her arm. It was better to remember that than to think about how delectable she looked.

She had changed, too, and was wrapped in a fleecy blue bathrobe. Idly he wondered what she had on underneath and choked on his sandwich.

"Are you all right?" She moved as if to come slap him on the back, and her robe gaped enough so he could see the lacy edge of a flannel gown beneath. He sucked in a deep breath.

"'M fine," he managed. "Just fine." He scalded his tongue on the coffee gulping it down. "Fine," he panted again, setting the cup on the table. "Just went down the wrong way."

She settled back against the sofa and picked up her sandwich. Silence descended once again. He tried to think of something to say, but he'd never been good at small talk at the best of times. And somehow he didn't think suggesting they catch the afternoon's college football scores on the late news would be a very good idea. Finally he brought up Tuck, mentioning the boy's enthusiasm for what Brenna had taught him. She responded.

And they got through the meal that way. But eventually even Tuck's talent ceased to be a viable topic, and then Brenna yawned.

"Sorry," she said, covering her mouth. But Jed took it as an excuse to gather up the paper wrappers and cups. It was late. They'd had a long day. She was probably exhausted. God knew he was. But he still refused to look at the bed.

"You want to play cards?"

"Cards?"

He flushed, feeling idiotic. "No, 'course you don't. You want to go to sleep. I'll...get out of your way." He grabbed his jacket off the chair and shrugged it on.

She sat up straight. "Why are you...*where* are you going?"

"Just out. For a walk."

"But—"

"I...need a little exercise." He heard the double sense of his words even as he said them, and his flush deepened. "Go to sleep," he said, and was out the door in one second flat.

He did need exercise—about ten thousand push-ups, a few thousand sit-ups, a five-mile run, then maybe he could cut down a few redwoods. That might put a damper on his desire. He shouldn't have brought her down here. He should have said, thanks, but no thanks, to the offer of a honeymoon. He should have said he had work to do. He should have had his head examined for suggesting marriage in the first place!

Well, smart guy, you didn't, he reminded himself as he slipped out a side exit, not wanting to chance the lobby and curiosity of Jenny's sister. *And now you're just going to have to cope.*

He'd learned to cope with Tuck in his life, hadn't he?

Yeah, sure. Like there was any similarity.

He started to walk. It was still snowing. The wind from the west knifed through him. He hunched his shoulders against it and kept going. It would be salutary, he told himself. It had the arctic ferocity he needed.

But what he really needed was exactly what he knew he could never have—Brenna naked and loving him in that big wide bed.

Get used to it, he told himself. It served him right, married to her and not daring to make love to her. He knew that.

But knowing it and experiencing it were two different things. It had been easy enough to tell himself about the extent of his willpower when it was an abstract notion. He should have remembered, he thought with grim humor, how little of it he really had. It was his lack, after all, that had caused him to leave her in the first place.

That and—

His fists clenched. His eyes shut.

He could still see her, warm and quite likely willing, her eyes smiling at him, welcoming him.

"Go for it, then," he taunted himself harshly, his words cutting as fiercely as the wind. "Go back there and make love to her. The doc said it was all right."

But it didn't matter what the doc said. The doc didn't know what he knew.

"Chicken," he called himself. Yes, in a word. Because it would open up a whole can of worms that didn't need opening. Raise issues he didn't want raised.

"Leave it alone," he said softly. "Just leave it alone."

He had more than he'd dared hope for in eleven long years. More than he had any right to expect. He had Brenna in his life once more. For now. Perhaps, if he was lucky, forever. For better or for worse.

Or both at the same time, he reckoned, if God had anything to say about it.

He glanced up and saw a lighted window and heard the sound of honky-tonk music. He'd take solace where he could find it tonight—even in a rough-and-tumble cowboy bar.

He stayed until closing. But the trio of straight whiskeys he downed didn't provide much solace.

He went back to the room and slipped in as quietly as he could. Brenna had left the light on in the bathroom, and in the faint spill of light he could see her silhouette on the far side of the king-size bed. He breathed a sigh of relief. She rolled over.

"Jed?"

He jerked. "What?"

She pushed herself up against the headboard to look at him. Her hair was tousled, and she looked exactly like he'd always imagined her looking in bed. He stepped back.

She shoved her hair away from her face. "You were gone a long time."

He shrugged. "Bein' cooped up doesn't agree with me."

"Are you all right now?"

"Sure. Fine," he lied.

"So, are you . . . coming to bed?"

"Bed?" The word stuck in his throat.

"You're going to have to sleep sometime." She looked up at him expectantly.

He swallowed. "Yeah, but—"

She smiled faintly. "If you're worried that I might . . . that I'd expect . . ." She stopped, flustered. Her hands twisted the bed covers.

"I'm not worried!" he blurted.

Brenna gave a soft, sudden exclamation and pressed a hand to the blanket covering her abdomen.

Jed frowned. "What's wrong? What'd I do?"

"Nothing. You didn't do anything. It just . . . kicked me. Hard." She looked up at him. "See."

And damned if she didn't lower the blanket that had been covering her breasts! The blue flannel, scoop-necked nightgown he'd glimpsed earlier was a soft tent over her unborn child. And her.

"God," Jed muttered.

"There it goes again." She laughed. "Can you see?"

He saw. Unable to stop himself, he ventured closer. Tiny thumping movements pulsed beneath the cotton. He stared, fascinated. He'd seen and felt the movements of unborn calves often enough. Hell's bells, he'd delivered more than he could count. But never this!

"Want to feel?"

Before he could back away, Brenna had grasped his hand and pressed it against her belly. It was hard and smooth, not soft and yielding, beneath his fingers. He'd barely registered his surprise, when it kicked him! Hard.

"Ho-lee!" An astonished grin broke out on his face and he lifted his gaze to meet hers.

It was the first genuine unstudied smile they'd shared in eleven long years. It wasn't at all like the strained ones they'd given each other at the wedding, or the awkward nervous ones they'd managed during the drive and during their meal.

Hers was the smile he remembered all too well. It was a smile that confided, trusted, shared. A smile that included him, offering an intimacy he'd once dared hope for.

Another tiny kick jolted him into action. He jerked away and stuffed his hands into the pockets of his jeans.

"Jed?"

"What?" He turned his back to her.

"We've never discussed the physical side of this marriage."

No, thank God, they had not. And they weren't going to now if he had anything to say about it. "What's to discuss," he said shortly. "You're gonna have a baby."

"But Jenny said the doctor said—"

"No." He kept his back to her.

There was a long silence. Then he heard Brenna sigh. "I understand," she said softly.

She didn't. She couldn't. And he couldn't explain. He didn't look at her, just stood stock-still, his fingers curling into fists.

"Of course, you're right," she said after a moment. "I just thought you might want—might need—"

"No!" he said vehemently. "I don't need anything."

"You're sure?"

Damn, any minute now he was going to crawl the blinking walls! "Yes." The word hissed through his teeth.

"All right," she said, but there was still hesitation in her voice. "But I would understand if you wanted..."

"I want a shower!"

He bolted then, shutting himself in the bathroom and locking the door as if he was afraid she'd come after him.

"And do what," he asked himself in disgust, "jump your bones in the shower?"

He wished. No, damn it, he didn't. Oh God. He pressed his forehead against the ceramic tile of the shower and tried to think calm, sensible thoughts. How the hell had he got himself into this?

He wondered if Madger and her nosy bureaucrats would be pleased if they could see him now.

Once upon a time Brenna had had dreams of a honeymoon with Jed. They'd been nothing like this.

She tried to tell herself it wasn't her he was rejecting. It was simply that she was so very pregnant he would feel awkward making love to her. Not to mention that the child who would literally come between them was the child of another man.

That was it—of course it was. She didn't blame him. And she took solace in knowing that, after the way he'd kissed her at their wedding, he wasn't completely indifferent. She supposed she shouldn't have been so forward to as to offer—

Her cheeks heated at the memory. But it wasn't as if she didn't realize that men had needs! Wasn't it better to acknowledge them? Maybe it was too soon. Jed was, after all, an old-fashioned man. Stubborn and idealistic as they came. He'd probably just want to "tough it out."

Brenna sighed and listened as he used half the water in the state of Wyoming before he finished his shower. Then she heard him brush his teeth, flick off the light and quietly open the door. She lay perfectly still, barely breathing, waiting to hear his footsteps approach the bed. Closeness, she told herself. At least she would have closeness.

Instead a moment later she'd heard him cross the room to the closet and take out the spare blanket and pillow. Then, to her amazement, he stretched out on the floor.

"Jed?"

She saw him stiffen. Then, "Go to sleep," he said.

"But you don't have to—"

"Yes," he said. "I do."

Stubborn cuss. She smiled slightly and folded her hands across her belly. The baby gave a tiny thump. *You approve, do you?* she asked it silently. She drew a breath and let it out slowly. Then she rolled onto her side so she could look down at him.

His back was to her. It didn't matter. Still she could watch him. Someday she would touch him. Someday he would touch her. Someday, perhaps, they would recover what they'd lost. Someday, she hoped, she would understand what had gone wrong.

For tonight, this was enough.

"Goodnight, Jed," she said softly. *I love you.*

There was a crack of light coming in between the closed drapes when she awoke. She opened her eyes slowly, lazily almost, started to smile, then looked down to see an empty rumpled blanket on the floor. She listened. No running water. No sounds at all. She sat bold upright. "Jed?"

Her heart was was pounding. An unreasoned panic seemed to clutch her.

And then, just as she imagined the worst, a key sounded in the lock and the door opened. Jed came in with fast-food bags clutched against his chest. He was dusted with snow and grimacing as he tried to keep the bags and coffee cups from falling while he quietly nudged the door shut with his toe.

Brenna's panic dissolved into love. He was bringing her breakfast in bed.

"Good morning," she said softly.

His head jerked around. "I didn't mean to wake you. I just figured you might get up hungry, so I went out and got some stuff." As he spoke, he was setting the items one by one on the nightstand: glasses of juice, muffins, cinnamon rolls, ham-and-egg-and-cheese sandwiches, two large cups of coffee.

"I didn't know what you'd want so—" he shrugged "—I got a little bit of everything." He gave her a quick smile. It was a shy smile, a tentative one. But real. Like the one they'd shared last night when the baby had kicked.

"It looks wonderful," Brenna said, smiling back and pressing her stomach now, not because of the baby but because of its own embarrassing growling. She swung her legs out and got up to put on her robe, then settled back in and dared to pat the edge of the bed. "Come sit down."

Jed hesitated, but only for a moment. Then he sat. Brenna took a muffin and handed him one. She settled back against the headboard. He perched on the edge of the bed. But gradually, as he ate his way through the muffin and the ham-and-egg biscuit sandwich, he seemed to relax.

"It's still snowing," he said. "Not hard, though." He got up to open the drapes so she could see. When he returned, she moved back to give him more room. He settled down more easily this time.

Brenna smiled. Progress. She licked the sticky cinnamon off her fingers. "It's good. You're taking very good care of me."

"I intend to." The look he gave her was solemn. The words were a promise.

She believed him. There had never been any question in her mind about Jed's sense of responsibility. If she hadn't insisted that it was her fault, he'd have owned up to causing her broken arm all those years ago. He'd always done what he thought was the right thing.

Hadn't he taken Tuck on when his sister died?

"Never hesitated," Taggart had told her one day last week when he stopped by to discuss cattle prices, and the talk later turned to his foreman, her fiancé.

"Same as he took care of his mother when she was sick. Marcy couldn't be bothered, but Jed was always there for her. Even after he'd worked the whole damn day. Your dad told him to take some time off, but he wouldn't. Said it wasn't what Otis was payin' him for." Taggart smiled. "He's a man you can count on to do the right thing. Even if it's the hard thing."

Unspoken, Brenna was sure, were the words that would say Jed's marrying her was "the right thing" and "the hard thing."

She understood. Jed's sense of commitment, his responsibility, his determination to do the right thing, were all part of the man she'd fallen in love with all those years ago.

She studied him now. He was so much, so very much, the same man he'd been then.

What had happened?

Brenna knew she couldn't ask him about it. This rapport they had was too new, too tentative. No, she couldn't ask. Not now. Maybe not ever.

Could they stay married for years and still have that lie unmentioned between them?

She didn't know.

She only knew that today they would. And maybe tomorrow. And after that, who knew?

They finished the rolls and muffins and drank the juice. Jed went out and brought back more coffee while Brenna got dressed.

Then they went to the museum.

It was really a historical center with four museums under one roof—one that contained memorabilia from Buffalo Bill Cody's Wild West Show, one that celebrated the culture of the Plains Indians, one that chronicled the development of firearms, and one that displayed a fine collection of Western art.

Brenna had seen and enjoyed them all before, but the art museum was her favorite, and not just because they had last year bought two pieces of her work.

"They did?" Jed said when she told him. Then, "They did!" he exclaimed as they came around the corner of one of the rooms that had contemporary art, and he stopped dead at the sight of the painting on the opposite wall.

It was a three-foot-by-four-foot canvas, larger than the ones she usually worked on. A pencil-and-watercolor piece of a cowboy rounding up horses.

It had all the elements her work was known for—the subtle earth tones that seemed somehow to bleed together—man and horses and landscape—with the sharp pencil edge that showed where one ended and the other began. It was the first she'd done of her Cowboy Heroes, the paintings for which she'd begun to receive recognition in the art world. The paintings showcased both her talent and the world she'd grown up in. They gave the cowboy a romantic tone, yet a hard edge.

This particular cowboy was the first she'd ever painted—the beginning of the series she'd begun right after she'd moved to New York. The subject was nostalgic, a way to stay in touch with her heritage. But the cowboy was incidental, she'd told herself at the time. She certainly hadn't lingered over him. He was just there at the back of a herd of mustangs, a shadowy presence.

It was only in subsequent paintings that he had become more defined, more detailed, more vivid. As the years had passed, her focus had shifted—from the land to the man. Though there was no getting away from the land, she had centered her energies on him, studied him, sought to understand the work he did, the life he lived.

As time passed, he became as real to her as the child she carried within her. And like that child, a part of him was still unknown, still hidden. In all the years she'd been painting him, she'd never shown his face.

It was what made him universal, the critics said. He was Every Cowboy. Every Man. One artist's tribute to An American Legend.

Brenna let them say what they would.

Jed moved closer now. Brenna hung back, watching him. She didn't care about the reactions of people who came to her gallery openings. She never painted to impress. She painted to remember, to capture, to evoke, not to be understood.

But she couldn't help watching Jed.

It was because he was a cowboy, she told herself. It was because he would be a true critic, someone who would know if she'd got it wrong. Or right.

If it was anything else, she wasn't ready to admit it.

He stood for a long time in front of the painting. He moved to the right and tipped his head. He stepped back. He shoved his hands in the back pockets of his jeans and rocked on the heels of his boots. People moved between him and her painting. They stopped and murmured; they talked as they pointed at this work and that. Jed didn't seem to notice. He approached the painting again, then stopped, still not speaking.

Brenna gave him plenty of room. She didn't speak, either. Or move. She only waited until at last slowly he turned and looked at her. Then something in his expression brought her out of her frozen state and she walked toward him.

"Yes," he said.

Just yes.

But the word—along with the light of respect in his eyes as he looked at her—was enough. She felt as if a weight had been lifted from her shoulders.

She smiled and he smiled back at her. They moved closer together.

A couple of children skittering past jostled them. They bumped together as they started to walk into the next room.

Their fingers touched. Brushed. Locked.

It might not be your standard regulation honeymoon, Brenna thought as they moved together through the museum, but things were looking up.

Eight

Jed knew his limits.

He could hold her hand the way he had in Cody at the museum. He could walk down the street with their shoulders brushing and her hair blowing in his face. He could even lay a hand on her abdomen when her child kicked within her and share a smile.

He could not share her bedroom night after night. Not and keep his sanity.

"But what will Tuck say?" she asked.

When he and the boy brought their belongings to the ranch house Monday night, Tuck immediately disappeared into the room Brenna had designated as his, but Jed stood in the middle of the hall, his arms full of clothes, and waited for Brenna to give him another option.

Any other option.

"Who cares what he says?"

"Nobody, I guess, but—" she gestured helplessly toward the room he knew was hers "—there is nowhere else."

He nodded toward the bedroom at the front of the house. "What about there?"

"That's my father's room. He's coming home on Wednesday. You can't put things in there."

Well, he could. But then he'd have to move again because Otis was, in fact, coming home. They'd gone to see Brenna's father earlier that afternoon to tell him about their marriage.

Even though he knew the old man wanted out of the nursing home, Jed had been prepared to have him object mightily to the means they were using to accomplish it. Eleven years ago Jed would have expected him to come after a hired hand who dared dream of marrying Otis Jamison's daughter.

So when Brenna said, "Daddy, Jed and I got married Saturday," he waited for the explosion.

Otis had squinted up at him for a long moment—so long that Jed had swallowed, tempted to look away—before he cleared his throat. "Finally," he said, and spat into his handkerchief. "Took long enough."

Jed had gaped at him, unable to respond.

Brenna had intervened. "Now there will be someone to help keep the ranch going," she said lightly, ignoring her father's words. "And you can come home."

"'Bout time," Otis muttered.

Jed was fairly sure he meant it was about time to come home, not that it was about time that Jed had married Brenna. But in either case, when he did, Otis wasn't going to look kindly on sharing a room with his new son-in-law.

"I could bunk with Tuck," Jed said.

Brenna just looked at him, her expression unreadable. "Fine. Bunk with Tuck," she said at last, then turned on her heel and went back down the stairs.

Oh, hell. He started after her.

Tuck poked his head out the door of his bedroom. "Hey, Jed. Come look at the neat desk Brenna set up for me. An' she's hung my pictures!"

Jed, torn between following Brenna and having another go at sticking his foot in his mouth or checking out Tuck's room, chose Tuck—for the moment at least.

He went into the bedroom. Tuck was beaming, his arms flung wide as he stood in the middle of what was undoubtedly the boy's dream room. Brenna must have been busy between the time they got engaged and the wedding. There was a pair of sturdy bunk beds, a wide uncluttered drawing table, a bookshelf with several art books already in residence and a solid old chest of drawers. Nothing fancy, but everything a boy like Tuck could want.

And there on the wall above the table, Brenna had hung the sketches Tuck had made of the branding. Including the one of Jed, stunned, on his rear in the dust.

About the way he felt right now.

He took his clothes into Brenna's room.

"I put my stuff in your room," he told her when he went downstairs. "But I'll sleep on the couch. It'll be better that way—for you. And for the baby."

Then he escaped altogether, heading for the barn on the thinnest of pretexts. He dawdled there, checking things out, messing with tack, picking out horses' hooves, until he was sure both Brenna and Tuck had gone to bed.

When he came back in, he found that she had made the couch up as a bed. Good, he thought. She had taken him at his word. He brushed off the faint hollowness he felt.

The couch was lumpy, bumpy and short. Though he wasn't quite six feet, the couch wasn't quite five ten. Still, he assured himself, he'd slept on worse. The couch in the cabin had been a wreck, and he'd slept there since Tuck had moved in. He'd be fine.

Or he would have been, if he hadn't passed Brenna's room on his way to take a shower.

He glanced in, he couldn't help himself. The overhead light was off. Only the small lamp by the bed was lit. The bed itself was empty.

Just then Brenna appeared, coming out of the small alcove where she'd set up the baby's crib. She tottered across the room toward the bed, her hands behind her, pressing against her lower back. As he watched, she lowered herself slowly, wincing, onto the edge of the bed.

"Are you all right?"

She looked up, startled. "Just tired. It was a long drive." She grimaced. "My back hurts."

"Can I do anything? Get you anything?" A pill, he meant. A hot-water bottle.

"You could rub it."

Jed stared at her, his mouth suddenly as dry as the Sahara. His heart kicked over like a galloping horse. *Rub it?*

Brenna smiled again, wryly this time, and sighed. "Never mind. I don't suppose it's in your job description. I shouldn't have suggested it."

"Job description?" Jed demanded, stung.

She shrugged. "You're supposed to run the ranch and be here so my dad can come home, right?" Her voice was soft and weary. "So you need your sleep. You have to be out early with Taggart, don't you?"

He and Taggart had planned to check the fences where both ranches bordered the National Forest, and keep an eye out for any cattle they might have missed in the roundup. "Winterizing," Taggart called it, because once the heavy snows began, any cattle left up there wouldn't be fed.

"Um," Jed said. "Yeah, but—" He still didn't move.

"That's what I thought. So go on. Good night." She raised her legs to slip them under the covers. She was wearing the same flannel nightgown she'd worn the night before, and he caught a glimpse of firm calves and a shadowed flash of creamy thighs.

"I'll rub your back," he said.

You're out of your mind, he told himself even as he crossed the room. But knowing didn't stop him. "Wh-where do you want me to rub?"

She rolled onto her side away from him, then raised a hand behind her, brushing it against her lower back. "Here."

There? Jed cleared his suddenly constricted throat. "Right," he muttered. Then, sucking in his breath, he knelt beside the bed.

Brenna supported herself on a pillow wedged against her abdomen and waited. Jed watched her back lift and fall with the breath she took. Then carefully he put his hands on the soft cotton covering her back.

Her body was warm through the brushed cotton of her gown. It was firm and resilient. Jed felt a stirring firmness of his own, low and insistent. He tried to will it away. Determinedly he concentrated on moving his fingers in slow rhythmic strokes up her back, then down. He tried to make his thumbs work diligently over the ridge of her spine, to knead, and not think about what—*whom*—he was kneading.

Brenna sighed, then made a soft whimpering sound.

"Does it hurt?"

"Not…at all. It's won-der-ful." Her voice was almost a purr. He felt like whimpering himself. He gritted his teeth, adjusted his jeans. Kept kneading.

Brenna sighed again. Her breathing slowed and deepened. God Almighty, was he putting her to sleep?

Jed shifted, craning his neck, trying to see if her eyes were open.

"Would you be more comfortable sitting on the bed?" she asked suddenly.

He jerked, his fingers clenching momentarily on the fabric of her gown. "What?"

"I just thought you might be uncomfortable on the floor. I can move over." She shoved the pillow as she said the words, inching over, leaving him plenty of room to sit next to her.

Jed swallowed a moan. *I'll stay where I am,* he started to say. But he couldn't reach her now that she'd moved.

He sucked in a breath, then sat on the bed. He put his hands on her back once more, shut his eyes and began to rub. She sighed and moved sinuously under his ministrations. His jaw clenched.

"Jed?"

"What?" His voice cracked.

"Do you think it's going to work?"

"What's going to work?" He sounded hoarse, even to his own ears.

"This. Our…marriage."

Oh God, not a heart-to-heart talk on top of everything else!

"Why wouldn't it?" he croaked. Determinedly he made his fingers knead their way up her spine, then back down. With his thumbs he pressed each vertebra. Sore muscles were a cowboy's specialty. Remember that.

"R-regular marriages often don't."

Did yours? He didn't ask, but he wanted to. He didn't know anything about her first marriage other than the few vague things Taggart had said about her sculptor spouse.

He could guess, though. Probably it had been everything this marriage wasn't. Real, honest, a joining of two people in love and not—

His fingers tightened involuntarily. "That's because they don't work at 'em," he said gruffly. "We'll work."

She took so long to answer he thought she'd gone to sleep. But then she said, so softly he could barely hear her, "Yes. Yes, we will."

She got everything he told her she'd get when she married Jed McCall. She got a conscientious cowboy who worked all day like a demon. A man who spent hours circling the range, checking fences, bringing down strays that had eluded them during the roundup, conscientiously doctoring cattle and moving cattle. When a heavy snowfall midweek left more than a foot of snow on the ground in the valley and he had to start feeding them, too, he didn't complain. He worked hard.

He worked hard with Tuck, too. Carefully and with patience he taught Tuck how to mend the porch railing. Determinedly, though with impatience at himself, he helped the boy with his math, struggling to remember what he'd been taught about long division. "Haven't had to use it in years," he confessed to Brenna afterward.

She was glad he hadn't asked her to help with that. He didn't. He only asked that she keep up the art lessons. She did—with pleasure. And Tuck continued to blossom.

Her father blossomed, too—mostly due to Jed's attention. If her father grumbled and fussed when she tried to get him to do something for himself, he was stoic and determined when

Jed suggested it. Consequently he made more progress in a few weeks around Jed than he had in months at the nursing home.

They talked, too. Man talk. Or rather Otis did. Jed listened. When her father went on and on about the cattle, Jed paid attention. When Otis talked about the history of the valley and how things were going to hell these days, Jed nodded his head. When Otis sent him to find the cribbage board in the cabinet in the dining room, then insisted they play every single night, Brenna wanted to protest that Jed needed some time to himself, but Jed never said a word and he played cribbage as if his life depended on it.

Perhaps it did. If his life depended on how much time he didn't have to spend with her, Brenna thought more than once.

It wasn't a fair thought and she chastised herself immediately. She had no right to expect more than he was already giving in this marriage. He was good with the ranch, encouraging with Tuck, patient with her father.

"Damn matches keep breakin'," she heard Otis fume as his trembling hand snapped yet another as he tried to put it in one of the holes in the cribbage board.

Jed flipped the head off another one and hand it to his father-in-law, waiting patiently while Otis fumbled it in.

"You could do it a damn sight faster," Otis grumbled, shooting Jed a dark look.

"But you wouldn't get any better," Jed replied with quiet frankness.

Their eyes met. Otis harrumphed and sputtered. Jed waited. And then play resumed, continuing until Otis finally made his way up to bed. By then it wasn't really that late, but because Jed had been up since before dawn, he was yawning.

"You should go to bed," Brenna said as she folded the newspaper and started to go up the stairs.

"I will," he said. "But first you gotta have your back rub."

Every night now he gave her a back rub.

A small thing, really. Insignificant. Yet to Brenna it represented everything she wanted and couldn't have.

It was, simultaneously, the most blissful and yet the most miserable moment of her day. It was the one time Jed touched her, the one time they were alone. The one part of their marriage that ever brought them into close contact.

And it stopped there.

Every night he sat on her bed and touched her. Every night he brought her bliss and a deep yearning ache. Every night he ran his hands over her, soothed her and softened her, stroked her and at the same time stoked the fires inside her. He made her dream, hope, desire.

And then he went away.

She should say no, she didn't want it. She should say, thank you, but her back was feeling fine. She didn't. She couldn't.

It was a small thing, that back rub. But it wasn't insignificant.

It was the only thing she had.

It was the only thing he had.

His chance, once a day, to touch her. To rub his hands over the flannel-covered skin that once he had touched when it was bare. To knead with firm, smooth strokes the flesh that once his trembling fingers had dared to caress.

It was agony. It was as close to ecstasy as he was going to get. And he was, apparently, a glutton for the punishment of having this much, no more.

"Jed?"

He hated it when she talked to him while he was doing it. They were too close for comfort. His control was too tenuous. There was no telling what he might be provoked to do—or say.

"What?" His response came on a harsh exhalation of breath and sounded far more abrupt than he intended.

He saw her swallow. "Never mind."

His fingers stilled momentarily. Then, with deliberation, he began to press and smooth her back again. "Sorry. I didn't mean— What do you want?" This time he sounded better, calmer.

"I—" she hesitated "—have a favor to ask. But I don't want to... take advantage."

"Ask." She couldn't ask him for anything harder than what he was already doing. "Would you come to birthing classes with me?"

"Birthing classes?"

"Before the baby comes. They teach you—me—" she corrected "—how to breathe and how to relax during labor. And I'm ... supposed to bring a coach."

"A coach," he repeated stupidly.

"To help. To rub my back." Her mouth tipped in another smile. "And you're very good at that."

"During your labor?" He seemed to be laboring over the mere words.

"Yes." She ran her tongue over her lips. "I guess Tess Tanner could do it if you don't want to. She is a nurse and she's had babies, so she'd be fine, really ..." Her voice faded and she looked at him hopefully.

Let Tess do it. He wanted to say it badly. He wanted to get up off the bed and back out of the room. He'd married her, yes, but he'd never agreed to go through her labor with her! He opened his mouth, then he looked into her eyes. Oh, hell.

Jed told himself there wasn't much difference between a woman having a baby and a cow having a calf. In theory he was probably right.

But, despite her increasing girth, Brenna didn't seem in the least bovine. And he didn't feel in the least like he was learning how to be midwife to a cow when he accompanied Brenna to the birthing class in Bozeman the following evening.

He felt awkward, out of place, nervous and eager to be someplace—*anyplace*—else. Just like nine-tenths of the fathers there.

"This your first time?" a weedy-looking guy with a goatee asked as Jed tried to fade into the wall he was leaning against. "Mine, too," the goatee said grimly. "I'm supposed to be into it. You know, be a useful liberated father and all." He shook his head. "Don't know how useful I'll be if I faint."

Jed wouldn't faint. He wouldn't let himself. He shoved himself away from the wall and went to kneel on the mat next to Brenna.

A nurse showed them a movie of a labor, giving them an idea what to expect, then showed them breathing exercises and set them to practicing.

"Deep, slow breaths," the nurse said. "You fathers, too. Breathe with them. Pace them. Put your hands on your wife's abdomen so you can feel for the start of the contraction and learn to control the breathing."

Jed's fists clenched on top of his thighs. "You're not having a contraction," he told Brenna.

"It's for practice," she said. "For control."

Feeling as if he was losing control, not gaining it, Jed settled back on his heels, adjusted his jeans, then laid his hands on the smooth taut skin of her belly.

"Breathe now," the nurse exhorted. "Slowly now. Slowly."

Jed ran his tongue over his lips, stared down at the belly beneath his fingers and breathed. Slowly. *Very* slowly.

The baby thumped against Jed's hands. He jerked back on his heels in surprise. "Wha—"

Brenna grinned. "Just saying hi."

Jed blinked, then a slow grin spread over his face. "Hi," he said softly.

He settled his fingers back against her, stilling their tremor against the soft cotton of the turtleneck shirt that covered Brenna and the baby both. There was another gentle flutter. He'd felt it move before, but he'd never considered it a person before.

Did that make him almost a stepfather?

"Christmas is coming and Brenna's getting fat," Tuck sang cheerfully as he dodged around her in the kitchen as she took the last batch of Santa cookies out of the oven. "Please to put a penny in the old man's hat." He cocked his head and considered her bulk. "You really are getting pretty humongous, you know."

"I know," Brenna said.

Thanksgiving was over. The snow was thick on the ground. They only had one more birthing class to go to. She was due in two weeks. And about time. She didn't walk anymore; she waddled. Going upstairs was only to be attempted if she knew she wouldn't have to come right back down. Painting was impossible. Not because of paint fumes—watercolorists didn't have to contend with those—but because she kept bumping into her belly every time she raised the brush and tried to bring it across her body. Then, too, being on her feet for any length of time made her miserable.

"It's about time for you to decamp," she'd told her passenger just the night before.

But when she thought about that, she felt something akin to panic. Her blithe assurances to Neil about how "of course she knew what she was doing," and "certainly she was capable of raising a child" seemed now to be so much hot air. "Whistling in the wind," her father used to call it.

Very soon now she was going to be called on to do far more than whistle.

And it wasn't only worry about her ability to cope with a new baby that set her panic wires humming, it was worrying about what was going to happen in her marriage—in her relationship to Jed.

So far against all odds they had survived—the strain between them that had existed in those first few days in Cody and at home had lessened. They had settled into a routine of sorts. Jed worked outside. She worked inside. They both spent time with Tuck and her father. Sometimes they spent time with each other. Cups of coffee in the morning, for example. Evening meals. Nights in front of the fire. Back rubs.

Brenna touched her back now and rubbed the ache that had been getting worse all day. Somehow, though, her fingers never did what Jed's could do and she wished he were here.

Fool, she called herself. But she wished it nonetheless. She knew she was living in a fairyland of sorts, relishing back rubs while skirting matters of substance—whole mine fields both past and present—that back rubs would never resolve. But Jed was skirting them, too. And in their mutual avoidance, they had achieved an equilibrium of sorts.

The baby's coming would change that.

Starting with the back rubs. She understood—was actually pleased with—his reluctance to make love to her at the moment. It showed concern, caring.

When circumstances changed—when they no longer risked hurting the baby, when she no longer resembled one of the cows—then things between them would change, too.

He might never want her the way he had obviously wanted Cheree, but she couldn't imagine him celibate forever. Within a few weeks he would want more. He would expect more.

They would make love.

Love?

Yes, Brenna thought, love. Even though she'd never said it aloud, even though she was quite sure he wouldn't want to hear it, she would be making love to him.

She wasn't sure when she had given up trying to fight it. She had admitted it to herself that first night in Cody. But she knew she'd felt it even longer—probably about the time she realized that her biggest enemy wasn't Jed, it was herself. Her feelings for him were so deeply rooted that no amount of time, good sense and logic could make them die.

So she would love him when the time came.

But would he love her? Ever?

She set the cookie sheet on the counter and reached a hand around to rub her back once more.

Suddenly the door banged open and there he was, lean and dark and as handsome as ever, his cheeks reddened with the cold, his hat dusted with new-fallen snow.

He frowned as she straightened and dropped her hand. "You all right?"

"Fine," she said brightly. "Just unwieldy. Tuck thinks I'm fat."

"I didn't mean it!" the boy protested, then grinned when he saw she was teasing.

Jed stepped back and assessed her with such thoroughness that Brenna found herself flushing, too. "You are a little porky," he agreed at last, then grinned when she swatted him with a dish towel. "You oughta sit down and put your feet up. How 'bout comin' for a little ride?"

"Don't you have work to do?" She wished she hadn't spoken, the moment the words were out of her mouth.

For once Jed said, "It can wait." He took her jacket off the hook by the door and spun her around, slipping her arms into the sleeves. "Come on." There was a suppressed excitement in him that she couldn't resist.

"I have to put my boots on." Getting past her belly made that such a challenge that, if it wasn't absolutely necessary, most days she didn't bother with shoes at all.

"I'll do it." Jed steered her toward the rocking chair at the far end of the room and pushed her down gently. "Tuck, bring me Brenna's boots."

Tuck brought the boots and Jed knelt before her. The brim of his hat bumped her knees and he reached up and tossed his hat aside, then bent to his task again, lifting her foot onto his thigh. Brenna watched him, mesmerized. A fringe of dark hair brushed against her this time, and she had to clench her fists to keep from reaching out to touch the short silky strands as she felt him slide her foot home.

"Now the other one," he said and slipped it on. Then he pushed himself to his feet again and held out a hand to her.

"A ride?" Brenna said, mystified and just a little shaky. It was the heat in the kitchen, she told herself. Not Jed. The baby began to push against her abdomen and she pressed a hand against it. "Where?"

Jed smiled. "You'll see."

He was still smiling as he ushered them out the door. "Hop in."

He didn't mean in the truck. He meant in the wagon. Her dad's old Belgians were hitched to the hay wagon, and Jed had left enough hay in the back to provide a reasonable cushion, then had covered it with a pair of old blankets. Brenna's eyes widened as he picked her up as if she weighed no more than Tuck, depositing her in the wagon bed.

He tucked a blanket around her, then said, "I'll be right back."

A few minutes later he returned with her father. Otis hadn't been out of the house since he'd come home five weeks ago. He'd made slow, steady progress though he'd grumbled through every bit of it. Come spring, Brenna imagined that he might be able to get out and around the ranch.

But now Jed was holding the door as the older man shuffled out onto the porch, and in his eyes Brenna saw an eager light that she hadn't seen in a long, long time.

"You sure 'bout this?" he asked Jed, his eyes flicking from his son-in-law to the seat of the wagon.

"I'm sure."

Brenna started to protest that her father couldn't possibly get clear up there. But before she could, Jed said, "Wait here." He climbed onto the wagon and circled the horses around the yard, bringing the wagon right next to the porch and stopping there. He handed the reins to Tuck. "Hold 'em."

Then he went back and helped Otis bridge the space between the porch and the wagon seat. Once Otis was settled, Jed hopped up, too, and took the reins from Tuck. "All set back there?"

At Brenna's reply, Jed made a clicking sound with his tongue and gave the reins a light snap. The Belgians moved slowly away.

He took them to cut a Christmas tree.

Brenna hadn't cut a Christmas tree since she was seven years old. The last time her father had bothered was the last year her mother had been alive. The three of them had gone together. A family.

And now she was going again. With her father. And Jed. And Tuck. And the child growing large inside her. A family? Was that what this meant?

The minute Jed stopped the team near the grove of evergreens, Tuck was off the seat and heading into the trees. Her father said he'd stay where he was, but the light remained in his eyes. Jed came around to the back of the wagon and waited to lift Brenna out.

She smiled at him as he swung her down. He smiled back. Then he slipped an arm around her, touching the very spot that had ached all day, and helped her up the hill.

Tuck wanted to take home trees so tall they'd have had to build another story on the house. He wanted to take home trees so fat they would have had to add another room. But finally the three of them agreed on a bushy spruce about eight feet tall. Jed sawed it down and he and Tuck prepared to haul it back to the wagon.

"I'll take you down first," Jed offered, but Brenna shook her head.

"I can make it."

Otis was beaming, but stamping his feet with the cold when they got there. He gave an approving nod to the tree they picked. "Reminds me of the ones your mother chose," he said quietly.

It was the first time in years Brenna could remember him mentioning her mother. The great love of his life, Leila Jamison had been so much a part of Otis Jamison's soul that he could barely talk about her without losing his tough facade. Consequently he almost never had.

Now Brenna nodded, her throat tight.

She was shivering by the time they got home. Her fingers felt icy in spite of her mittens, and her teeth wouldn't stop chattering even after she was back in the house.

Jed's face was a mask of consternation. "You should have said." He helped her into the house and tucked her into the chair by the fireplace. "I didn't realize."

Brenna took his equally cold hands in hers and squeezed them. "It was a wonderful idea. Tuck was thrilled. My father looks better than I've seen him in months. And—" She couldn't help herself. She pulled him down so that she could press a quick kiss against his cold mouth. "I wouldn't have missed it for the world!"

Back when Jed had still had dreams, he'd had big ones. A world champion bull-riding title. A ranch of his own— thousands of acres of prime Montana grazing land and cattle wearing a J-bar-M brand. A life with Brenna—a life filled with passion, romance and not a little love.

Some time ago he'd given up on dreams.

The bull-riding went first, about the time the ligaments in his knee did. He could still ride, but he wasn't world-class.

The ranch went next. He made it all right from paycheck to paycheck, but there was never much left over. And when the Hollywood types began buying up whatever land was available, well, he wasn't going to be able to run very many J-bar-M cattle on the twenty-odd acres he could afford.

And Brenna?

He'd left that dream behind a long, long time ago. Had destroyed it all by himself.

But now, unbelievably, God had given it back.

Not the grand passion, not the romance. God certainly knew Brenna had no reason to love him. But one way or another, Jed had one of his dreams. A softer, gentler version of it, perhaps. Not the life with Brenna he had once envisioned, but a life with Brenna nevertheless.

And it was a good life, too. A life made up of little things— those morning cups of coffee before anyone else was awake; those trips down to Bozeman where once a week they breathed together and he got to feel the fullness of her belly beneath his hands; the hundred percent on Tuck's math test that they all celebrated with root beer floats; the increasing number of steps Otis could manage easily every morning when he came downstairs; the thumbs-up from Madger the Badger when she'd paid them a visit last week and had smiled as she'd said she wouldn't be back anymore; the baby who leapt in Brenna's womb whenever Jed touched her; the nightly back rubs that left him hard and Brenna soft and sighing.

Yes, it was a good life.

He shouldn't want more.

But he did.

He told God he was sorry. He told God he knew he was being an ungrateful wretch who wanted more than he had any right to expect, certainly more than he deserved. He told God to stop him thinking about her that way.

But God didn't stop him.

So every night after he rubbed Brenna's back, Jed retreated down the stairs to the sofa where he slept and thought about making love to his wife.

He thought about easing the gown up her thighs and running his fingers along the length of her legs. He thought about slipping it over her head and caressing her breasts with his fingers, with his lips, with his tongue. He thought about feathering kisses across the flesh that leapt beneath his touch. He thought about touching the very core of her.

And tonight the urge was worse than ever because tonight she had kissed him. She'd made him remember all too well what it was like to let their mouths linger and savor each other. She had so fed his fantasies with memories long-and-determinedly buried, that even now, one decorated Christmas tree, twenty math problems, three cribbage games and one exquisitely tormenting back rub later, he still ached for the touch of her.

He moaned and twisted on the narrow couch. *Don't think about it,* he told himself. *Stop me,* he told God.

But he couldn't, and God didn't, so the torment went on and on.

He replayed the first date he'd taken Brenna on. He skipped over the movie, which had been eminently forgettable, and went straight for the slow drive back to the ranch which had not.

He remembered the way he'd eased an arm behind her, inch by calculated inch, then moved to draw her close. He remembered the way she'd slid across the seat to press against him, hip to hip. He remembered the soft cinnamon scent of her shampoo when the breeze blew her hair across his cheek. He remembered tangling his fingers in it. He remembered stopping the truck at the last gate and not getting out to open it. He remembered kissing her.

He remembered it all. The first date and every one after it. The eager kisses, the desperate gropings, the fevered flesh of both her body and his. He remembered petal soft skin and faint golden freckles. Sleek silken thighs and softly rounded breasts.

He remembered his mouth touching those breasts, remembered her shiver, then laugh and tug on his hair.

"Jed!"

He jerked at the very real, very urgent sound of her voice.

Then he realized it wasn't a dream. Brenna was standing silhouetted halfway down the stairs.

"Jed," she said more loudly, and he realized it wasn't the first time she'd spoken.

Wincing, he sat up. "Somethin' wrong?"

"I think I'm having the baby."

Nine

"**B**reathe," Jed said. It was as automatic as it was idiotic.

Brenna laughed. "I am." She took a deep breath just to show him. Then she laughed again. It was a nervous laugh. At least it made him nervous.

"You're not kidding?"

She shook her head. "I'm not kidding."

Intellectually, of course, he knew she had to have it sometime. But now that its arrival was imminent, he just sat there, disbelieving. It didn't matter that she was as big as the barn. It didn't matter that her belly kicked him when he put his hands on it. It didn't matter that he'd convinced himself he was ready for stepfatherhood.

When it was real, it was a different story.

"Breathe," Brenna suggested in the face of his stupefied silence.

It was a moment before he did. Then he got up and turned on a light. She looked pale, ethereal. He suddenly remembered that women had been known to die in childbirth. It galvanized him.

"Get dressed," he said harshly. "No, don't. Just put on a robe. I'll carry you to the truck."

"I can get dressed," Brenna said calmly. "And I can walk. Relax, Jed. We have plenty of time."

"How do you know? Have you ever done this before?" He shot her a hard glare over his shoulder. He had kept his back to her since he'd turned the light on. The desire he'd felt was fading fast, but he didn't want her seeing what was left before he got himself zipped up. He winced as he did it, then buttoned his jeans and fumbled to buckle his belt. Shrugging on his shirt, he went to wake Otis and Tuck.

"You'll be able to manage?" he asked Otis. "I can call Taggart if you want."

"We'll be fine, won't we, son?" Otis said. He'd come out of his room and was leaning heavily on Tuck's young shoulder.

Tuck nodded, but his eyes were round and worried as he looked up at his uncle. "She's havin' it now? Really? Wow."

Which was pretty much the way Jed felt.

The door to Brenna's bedroom opened and she came out, her hands pressed against her belly. "They've stopped."

"Stopped?"

"The contractions. Maybe it's a false alarm. I'm not due for another week, you know."

"How long did you have them before you called me?"

"A couple of hours." She rubbed at her back. "I'll just go sit down."

"Sit in the truck. We're going to the hospital."

"But if it's a false alarm I'll look like an idiot!"

"You'll look like a bigger idiot if you have it here. Say I forced you." Jed grabbed her packed suitcase and took her arm. "Call the doc and tell him we're coming," he told Otis.

The night was cold but clear as they started out. He thanked God for that. He'd wondered if he'd have to make the run in the middle of a blizzard. He was glad he did not.

"They've started again," Brenna said suddenly.

Jed's foot hit the accelerator. "Oh, God."

In fact he had time for plenty of prayers before things got really serious. While he answered questions in Admitting,

Brenna was whisked off to the maternity ward. The damn papers took forever, and Jed was gnashing his teeth by the time the boot-faced old biddy at the desk finally let him go.

He half expected Brenna to be in delivery when he skidded to a halt outside the labor room, but she was sitting in a chair reading a magazine. She looked up at him and smiled at him, and he felt suddenly awkward.

"At least they didn't send you home."

She shook her head. "Apparently this is the real thing."

He swallowed. "You ready?"

"Guess I'll have to be."

"Did the doc see you? How long does he think it will be?"

"He doesn't know. First babies are notoriously unpredictable." She hesitated. "If you don't want to stay—"

"Of course I'm staying."

She flushed. "It...might be a while. I didn't know. I thought maybe you'd want to go home...check on Tuck..."

"Tuck's fine," Jed said firmly. "Nothin's going to happen your dad can't handle. Unless—" now it was his turn to hesitate "—you changed your mind? I can call Tess."

"No. I want you," she said, just as fiercely as he'd said, "I'm staying." Her fingers tightened on the magazine. "I do," she repeated. "As long as it's what you want, too." She looked at him intently.

"It is," he said and felt as if they'd taken vows. A determination settled on him. He drew himself together, then hunkered down and smiled up into her eyes, reaching out and taking her hands in his. "Time to breathe."

She lost track of time. She lost track of place. She lost track of everything—but Jed.

He kept her focused. He held her hands and rubbed her back and sponged her forehead. He talked in low, steady tones that made more sense than all the nurses put together.

She had expected to cling to Neil's memory during these intense hours. And Neil was certainly there in spirit. But Jed was the one she hung on to physically and emotionally, the one she depended on to get her through.

When the time came to move to the delivery room, the doctor looked at Jed. "You up to this? I don't want to be reviving you."

Brenna shot him a quick worried glance, but his fingers tightened on hers, giving her a steady reassuring pressure.

"Let's go," Jed said.

He was as good as his word. He sat at the head of the delivery table and held her hands the whole time—her anchor, the port in the storm that swirled around her, the voice of steady encouragement she relied on. It was Jed's face she saw most clearly when, at eight-fifteen in the morning, her daughter entered the world.

"My God," Jed said as the wrinkled red infant came into the world. His tone was pure reverence. So, Brenna could see, was the expression on his face. Then he looked down at her.

"Oh, Brenna," he said. They both looked at the tiny perfect child and then back at each other. Jed swallowed, swiped a hand across his eyes and grinned. He squeezed her hands. With what little strength she had left, she squeezed back.

"We did it," she said softly.

He made a sound that was half laugh, half sob. "You did it."

She shook her head and said with perfect honesty, "I couldn't have—not without you."

He bent his head then, and dropped a gentle upside-down kiss on her lips.

I love you, she told him with her eyes, with her heart. *I do so love you.*

He didn't leave her until she told him she was fine, that it was all right to let go of her hands, that it was, in fact, probably a good idea for him to go call her father and Tuck.

"You're sure?" At her nod, he loosed her fingers and stood up. "Let's see. She's seven pounds five ounces, twenty inches long, brown hair and a lot of it—" he grinned "—and blue eyes. What else? Oh yeah. What are you going to name her?"

"I thought...Neile."

"Neile." He said the name matter-of-factly, but she heard a hollowness, a hoarseness in his tone. An ache that told her that she'd left explanations long enough. He started to turn away.

She caught his hand. "Go call them now. But when you come back we have to talk. I want to tell you about Neil."

He shook his head. "It's not my business."

Her fingers tightened on his wrist. "It is. And I want you to listen."

He didn't want to know.

He'd just shared one of the most intimate experiences a man can share with a woman, and he didn't want to hear about the man who should have been there instead.

But it didn't matter what he wanted right now. It was Brenna who had been through the stress of childbirth. It was Brenna who needed to talk about the man who had given her such a beautiful daughter.

It was his job—his penance, perhaps—to listen.

She was sitting up in bed when he came back nearly an hour later. She'd brushed her hair and was wearing the soft flannel nightgown he remembered from the torturous back rubs. She looked pale and tired, all except her eyes. There was life and happiness in her eyes.

"Did you tell them?"

He nodded. He stood at the foot of the bed, his fingers tightening around the metal of the foot rail. "I called Taggart and Mace and Noah, too. Taggart will bring Tuck and Otis down this afternoon, if you're up to it."

"Of course."

"You want to get some rest, then," he said, backing toward the door.

"No. I want to talk."

"But—"

She held out a hand to him. He had no choice but to come around the side of the bed and take her fingers in his. For a long moment neither of them spoke. Then, "Pull up a chair," she said.

He snagged one. He would have kept his hand out of her grasp then, but she took it back as soon as he was seated. Her fingers played with his, and neither of them spoke.

"You don't have to," he said with some urgency.

She rubbed her thumb across his knuckles. "I do," she said. "Neil was my best friend." And then she started to talk.

He listened because he had no choice. He listened because she wanted him to hear, to understand. He didn't want to. He was afraid to. But he listened.

"He was one of the most talented men I've ever known, an incredible sculptor. He found life in wood and in stone. In trash that other people threw out. He was also one of the most generous people I've ever known. He never belittled anyone else's work. He supported me in mine."

Jed's jaw tightened.

But Brenna didn't notice. She went on. "He gave me room to work in his studio. He introduced me to gallery owners. He got me my agent. He displayed my paintings on the walls of his apartment."

"*His* apartment?" Jed couldn't help asking.

"We didn't live together until after we were married. Before then we were *friends.*"

"He was more than your friend."

"Yes, but—not the way you're thinking." And then she told him about Neil getting sick. She told him the way Neil felt about his sculpture, that it was hard and cold.

"It's beautiful," Jed protested, because he'd seen some pieces she had back at her studio on the ranch. Smooth obsidian, rough wood. She was right. Neil found life where other people would overlook it.

"Yes," Brenna agreed. "But when he looked at his life, Neil felt that his sculpture wasn't enough." She let go of Jed's hand then, plucking the blanket, and he felt bereft. His hand felt lonely, cold.

"I knew he wanted a child." She watched her fingers crush the fabric in her hand. "So I suggested we get married."

"*You* suggested?"

She raised her eyes to meet his defiantly. "It made as much sense as me marrying you."

Stung, Jed nodded. "Yes. But..." He hesitated, then had to ask, "You didn't love him?" He could barely get the words out.

"Of course I loved him!" Her tone was fierce and her eyes flashed, but as soon as she said the words, her gaze dropped again. "I loved him," she repeated, "but not the way I—" She stopped suddenly and shook her head.

Not the way she... what?

Not the way you ought to love the man you married? Not the way she loved someone else? Not the way she loved *him?*

Oh, dear God. He shut his eyes for an instant, then opened them and looked deeply into hers. He still saw defiance there. He thought he saw something else as well.

Did he *want* to see something else?

"We were best friends. But we wouldn't have married if he hadn't become ill. That wasn't the sort of relationship we had. But I wanted him to have what he wanted, if it was possible. I knew if it happened, if I got pregnant, I would love his child." She stopped and looked away out the window. It had started to snow.

Jed barely registered it. He was busy trying to sort out what she'd told him.

She'd loved Neil, but... they were only friends. She'd loved Neil but...she hadn't wanted to marry him. She'd married him to have his child because he'd wanted it...

But it hadn't been a love match.

A tiny bit of the ice around his heart began to melt.

"I just...wanted you to understand how it was," Brenna said faintly, still not looking at him. She hugged her arms across her breasts.

Jed covered one of her hands with his. She turned it in his and their fingers curved around each other's. Tightened. Clung.

"Thank you," he whispered.

He stayed with her until she slept, watching her, loving her. He could have sat there all day, just looking at her, savoring the moment. But the nurse came in, smiled and said, "Why don't you go get something to eat while she's resting?"

He eased his fingers out of Brenna's, got up and stretched. His knees cracked. His back ached. He felt a hundred years old—except somewhere, deep inside, he felt newborn.

When he passed the nursery, his steps slowed. Stopping, he looked in.

There were only three babies, each with its name pasted in big letters above the isolette in which it lay. Jacob Robert Updegraf was on the left. Ashley Kathleen Miller was in the center.

And on the right, in brand-new pink letters, he read—Neile Sorensen McCall.

Neile Sorensen *McCall?*

Jed stared at her name. And at his. *McCall.* Somehow he hadn't thought . . . hadn't dared hope . . .

He swallowed, his throat tight. He blinked rapidly as he leaned his head against the glass and stared at the sleeping child—Brenna's child. And Neil's.

And his.

I hope you won't regret this.

They were among the last words Neil said to her before he died. He'd been getting weaker and, it seemed, she'd been getting stronger as the days went by.

"It's the way it should be," he'd said to her, pressing a hand against her still only barely rounded belly. She was showing no visible signs of pregnancy yet—other than throwing up every morning. Neil hated that more than she did. He wanted her to blossom. He was far happier during the rest of the day when she did.

"It's not the way it should be," Brenna had argued. "You shouldn't be dying."

But he was, and they both knew it.

While he was still strong enough, they walked every afternoon in Central Park. When he wasn't, she helped him out on the terrace of the third-floor brownstone floor-through where they lived. He wouldn't go to the hospital.

"They can't help," he said.

"Maybe they could make you more comfortable."

"You make me comfortable." He'd taken her hand and held it. The soft May sun caressed his pale face, giving him the lean, stark beauty of some of his sculptures. "Unless you want me to go." He searched her face. "Is this too hard on you?"

"No. Oh, no."

So he had stayed home until the end.

In the end it was quiet. Or as quiet as New York City ever was. He couldn't go outside anymore. He was too weak. But his bed was by the window and when he was awake he watched her paint or he looked out the window and watched the jets fly overhead.

"Brenna?" he'd said that last afternoon. It was the first time he'd spoken that day.

She was painting, though she'd spent hours earlier simply sitting beside him, tracing his features, committing them to memory as she held his hand. At the sound of his voice, she set down her brush and hurried to his side.

"Can I get you something?"

He shook his head, and his fingers reached for her. She took his hand. Neil had always had such strong hands. Now they closed over hers weakly. His blue eyes fluttered shut, and she thought he'd gone back to sleep. But then he opened them again.

"I love you," he said softly. His hand went out and, with what little strength he had left, he touched the front of the shirt she wore. His fingers grazed her abdomen. "Both of you."

Tears pricked behind Brenna's lids. "We love you, too."

He smiled and sought her hand again. Their fingers locked, and that's when he said, "I hope you don't regret this." He looked at the place where the child he would never live to see was growing inside her.

"I won't regret it, Neil," she'd promised and touched her lips to his.

An hour later he was gone.

Six and a half months later Brenna had a lot of feelings welling up inside her as she held her daughter in her arms and nursed her for the first time—but regret wasn't one of them.

She traced the baby's soft pink features. They were nothing at all like the stark gaunt features of her father in the last days of his illness. But Brenna thought that someday she would have Neil's smile, and her pale lashes and the light dusting of fair hair would likely recall Neil's own.

There was nothing hard and cold about Neile Sorensen McCall. She was precisely the legacy her father had wanted.

"She's beautiful," Brenna whispered now as a tear slid down her cheek. "Just beautiful, Neil. We'll do our best for her—all of us. Even Jed."

Neil had understood about Jed and, to his credit, he'd never tried to talk her out of her undying devotion to a man who had rejected her.

"How could I, when I feel the same way about you?" he'd asked her once with just the hint of a twinkle in his eye.

"You'd appreciate the irony of all this," she told him now, a faint smile curving her lips. But as she cuddled their daughter closer, she didn't think she had to tell him.

She was sure he knew.

If Madger the Badger could see them now, Jed thought, she'd be over the moon.

Tuck was sprawled on the floor, a drawing pad in front of him as he painstakingly sketched the Christmas tree and just-opened gifts; Otis was sitting in the rocker by the fire, his granddaughter cradled in his arms as he rocked her and crooned the cleanest verses of an old cowboy song; Brenna was humming in the kitchen as she put the finishing touches on the crust of a pumpkin pie and put it in the oven. When she took off her apron Jed saw a streak of flour in her hair and a smudge on the end of her nose. She looked far more tempting than the pie.

It was all he could do not to get up off the couch and cross the room to kiss it away. He didn't because—as he reminded himself daily and for what seemed a hundred times a day—that wasn't what this marriage was all about.

It was about satisfying Madger. It was about saving the ranch and giving Tuck and Neile two parents and Otis a place to come home to. And they'd done it. All of it. Every bit.

He should be glad.

He *was* glad.

It should be enough.

It *was* enough, Jed told himself sharply. But she was half-way across the room now, coming to sit down on the couch alongside him, and he ought to be heading for the door. But as she sank down beside him and nudged up against him, he found his arm going around her instead. He breathed deeply of the soft scent that was Brenna.

He could still resist. He would resist. Later.

Thank God they were going to Taggart and Felicity's for dinner. There would be more than a dozen people milling around to watch and listen to. He wouldn't be aware of Brenna's every move. And after dinner he would be able to escape into the den and play cards with Taggart and Mace and Noah same as he'd done last year. So he wouldn't have to watch her, wondering if she was getting tired—it had only been two weeks since she'd had the baby, after all—and she needed to rest.

He wouldn't have to play cribbage with Otis, either. Taggart's dad, Will, would undoubtedly be willing to keep Otis company. The old man wouldn't even miss him. He wasn't sure Will would have the patience to let Otis move his own matchsticks, though. Still, that wasn't his problem.

Not even Tuck would be a problem. He might insist on the five of them sitting around the living room together playing cards and drawing and telling stories and just generally "acting like a family"—Tuck's words—when they were home, but when he was with Becky and Susannah he'd have lots of other things to keep him busy. And if the three of them couldn't entertain themselves, they could take care of the little kids—Clay and Scott, and, of course, Neile.

Neile. Jed wouldn't have to be bothered with her, either. There would be so many people wanting to hold a new baby he wouldn't have to walk her around after Brenna fed her. He wouldn't have to rock her to sleep or drop kisses on her downy head tonight. Hell, there'd be so many kids making noise that he probably wouldn't even hear her cry.

No, he'd be fine tonight. Nobody needing him, nobody depending on him. Nobody caring if he was there at all.

Absolutely.

Neile was definitely the child of the hour.

None of the other kids was slighted, of course. Tuck and

Becky and Susannah, the "big kids," were far too busy to want to be doted on. Clay was content to stack blocks and knock them down again. Even Scott was mobile enough to wriggle when some misguided adult got the notion to cuddle a child.

But Neile loved every minute of it.

From the moment they walked into Taggart and Felicity's home that evening Brenna had almost never had a chance to hold her.

"Let's give your mommy a rest, shall we, sweetheart?" Felicity cooed, swooping down to take Neile out of Brenna's arms. "Don't you think another little girl would be nice, Taggart?"

Her husband came to peer over her and grin down into Neile's crossed eyes. "Either one would be fine with me. Or both." He reached around and rubbed Felicity's tummy and grinned.

Brenna's eyes widened. "Are you . . . ?"

Taggart's grin widened even further. "That's what the rabbit says."

"Taggart! They don't use rabbits anymore! It's what the litmus paper says," Felicity told Brenna, but she looked just as pleased.

"How wonderful!"

"I thought I could get in a little practice, if you don't mind," Felicity said. But she didn't get much before Tess came to claim her turn.

"My babies aren't babies anymore," she complained and took Neile away. "Look, Noah, don't you think a girl would be nice next?"

Noah Tanner looked from his tall brown-haired daughter to his small dark-haired sons and raised his eyebrows. "You want another one?"

Tess dimpled. "Or two."

Noah groaned. "It's so much work! But, hey—" he grinned "—what a guy's gotta do, a guy's gotta do. Why don't you put that kid down, and let's go home and get to work right now?"

Tess blushed and cuddled little Neile closer. "Later," she promised and batted her lashes in a way that made Noah blush, too.

Everyone else took a turn with Neile after that. Taggart's mother, Gaye, demanded surrogate grandmother rights. Jenny Nichols held her and rocked her to sleep with Mace looking on wordlessly. Otis demanded that he be allowed his nightly rock even though Neile was already asleep. And Will said every child deserved two grandfathers, so he reckoned he could take a turn, too.

Even Taggart and Noah held her. Taggart said he wanted to see if he could remember Becky ever being that small, and Noah, giving his own ten-year-old daughter a hug, said he couldn't imagine Susannah had ever been that small, and he was sorry he'd missed it.

Everyone held her. Except Jed.

He stood against the wall and glowered. At Brenna. But even more astonishingly, at the baby.

Brenna couldn't figure it out. He helped her at home with the baby. He was a little awkward at first, but in the past ten days he'd learned to change Neile and rock her, and twice he'd even got up in the night with her when Brenna was so tired that she could barely function. In short he did everything a new father was supposed to do.

Except dote in public.

It wasn't in the contract, she thought. When there were other people around to take care of her and Brenna, he let them.

At this very moment he was standing on the far side of the room, leaning against the wall, shoulder-to-shoulder with Mace Nichols, both of them looking as if their last name ought to be Scrooge, while Jenny sang funny little songs to the baby.

Neile was an easy baby most of the time, and never more so than tonight. No sooner had Brenna thought it, than Neile's patience ran out. Her face crumpled and she began to cry.

Brenna started to say, "Do you want me to take her?" But she didn't get half the sentence out before Jed was across the room and snatching Neile out of Jenny's arms.

"She's tired. And hungry." He looked at Brenna. "Let's go."

Brenna's eyes widened. Then, she nodded. "I'll just call Tuck," she said.

While she did and helped her father with his jacket, Jed continued to walk the floor with Neile, one big hand curved against the back of her tiny back and head to hold her snug against his chest and shoulder.

At first she kept crying. Then she whimpered and gummed her fist. Jed walked, murmured, rubbed her back. Finally a sigh shook her. Then another faint whimper. Her eyes shut. The room was silent.

"He's got the touch," Taggart said, awed.

Noah looked at him with respect.

"All set." Brenna held out her arms and, with obvious reluctance, Jed relinquished his burden to pull on his own jacket. Then he took her back and tucked a fleecy bunting around her as he settled her in the car seat and picked it up.

The entire assembled crowd watched.

He glared at them. "Somethin' the matter?"

They shook their heads.

"Not a thing, Jed." Felicity smiled conspiratorially at Brenna. They all did. "Not a thing."

Jed made a huffing sound. Brenna smiled.

Thank-yous said, dishes packed, they all trundled out to Otis's Suburban and piled in.

"Best Christmas ever," Tuck mumbled as he settled in and drifted against Otis's shoulder. "Huh, Gran'pa?"

In the front Brenna looked at Jed. Jed looked at Brenna. *Gran'pa?*

Apparently so, for Otis cleared his throat and edged an arm around the boy's narrow shoulders. "You got that right, son. It sure has been one of the best."

Yes, it had, Brenna thought, because she had a whole new take on Jed's wall-propping behavior. Far from being indifferent, he'd been playing watchdog the whole time. It wasn't that he didn't care, he cared a lot. About Neile.

What about her?

She had no right to ask. No right to even wonder. But looking at him out of the corner of her eye, she couldn't help it.

When they got back to the ranch, Jed helped her get every-one and everything into the house, then went to check on the animals. Brenna changed Neile, supervised Tuck's teeth brushing and face washing, then kissed him good-night, and then went to say good-night to her father.

He was sitting up in bed reading when she came in carrying Neile. He looked up at her and smiled, then patted the side of the bed and she sat down. He held out his arm for the baby and she placed Neile in the crook of his arm.

He rocked his granddaughter lightly, then looked down into the baby's face. "You're going to be a looker," he told her. "Just like your ma."

"Oh, Dad!"

"She is!" Otis maintained. "A man knows these things." He gave a sharp nod. "Good thing she'll have an older brother to keep the cowboys away. Except the right one, o'course." His eyes twinkled as he looked at her over the top of his glasses.

Brenna, flustered, looked away.

Otis reached out with his free hand and caught hers. "He is the right one, isn't he, sweetheart?"

Brenna shrugged. "I don't know," she said miserably. "I want . . . I hope—but—"

"He loves you."

"Does he?" Brenna wasn't at all certain. "I thought so once."

Otis loosed his hand from hers and brought it up to touch her chin, tipping her face so that she looked at him. "I did, too."

"Then why—?" She couldn't quite keep the anguish out of her voice.

"I don't know. Maybe you should ask him."

"I can't. Cheree—" She'd never said that to anyone before, especially not to her father.

Otis sighed. "Cheree."

He hadn't been married to Milly, Cheree's mother, for long. He'd missed Brenna's own mother so much and had been a widower so long that Brenna hadn't ever thought he'd marry again. And then one day he'd come home from a stock sale in Denver with a wife!

Milly was a gorgeous, birdlike city creature he'd met in the bar at the Brown's Palace Hotel. She was completely smitten with Otis. He was equally smitten with her. It had been a match of opposites—and it hadn't lasted.

Just long enough for her daughter Cheree to show up—and take Jed away from Brenna.

Only for a night, Brenna admitted to herself. Cheree had left a few days later. Jed had stayed on the ranch. But it must have been some night! He'd never looked at Brenna again.

"He never loved Cheree," Otis said, "whatever happened between them." He dropped a kiss on his granddaughter's head, then leaned forward and gave his daughter's cheek a gentle kiss. "He's a good man, Jed McCall, despite Cheree. He's proud and almighty stubborn, but he loves you." Otis nodded, a smile touching his lips. "A man knows these things."

Ten

If he loved her, he had a funny way of showing it.

Jed wasn't simply stubborn and proud. Once Christmas was over, he was as distant and remote—with her, at least—as when he'd dumped her eleven years before.

He was good with the baby—in fact he positively doted on her—but with Brenna he seemed more aloof than ever. He didn't look at her when they talked. He stood up if she sat down. He backed out of rooms almost as soon as she came into them.

And yet . . .

Sometimes, when he thought she wasn't looking, Brenna caught him watching her. It wasn't much to go on—a look. But there was such longing in that look. Such need.

She knew it well enough. She'd looked at him the same way for years.

So why didn't he do something about it? They were married! If he needed her, *wanted* her, what was stopping him?

Other than the fact that they had to wait until six weeks after the baby's birth before Brenna would be healed enough to make love, she couldn't think of one.

Was that the problem? Was Jed keeping his distance because, if he didn't, he wouldn't be able to keep his hands off her? Once Neile was six weeks old, would he come to her with all the longing she saw in his eyes?

She dared to hope.

In the meantime she nearly went crazy with longing herself.

She found release where she'd always found it—in her painting. While Neile napped and Tuck was at school, while Jed was wherever Jed had gone to escape her, she painted.

Loren, who had almost despaired of her ever working again, was thrilled.

"I need three more paintings before your show in February," he told her. "Can you do that?"

To save her sanity, yes, Brenna could.

"Of the cowboy?" Loren said. "The roping, riding, branding guy. Surely you've seen one or two since you've gone back. What else do they do?"

They coach childbirth, Brenna could have told him. They change diapers and rock babies. They help little boys with long division and short stories. They play cribbage with old men. They give back rubs.

"You'd be surprised," she said.

"So," Tuck said, leaning against the side of the truck, watching Jed's every move, "it's workin' out pretty good, wouldn't you say?"

Jed was concentrating on Otis's Suburban. He had his old truck figured out and he knew enough to put gas in Brenna's when it died. But Otis's Suburban was an entirely different kettle of fish. It had a computer for one thing. And an automatic transmission. And fuel injection. Hell, if he'd wanted to be a mechanic, he'd have cowboyed in Texas where they had windmills!

He'd take horses any day of the week. But the car had a problem, and Jed was trying to diagnose it before he had to pay someone else to do it. He didn't need distractions. "What?"

"Your marriage," Tuck said to clarify.

Now there was a distraction for you.

Jed had told himself that once Brenna had the baby, he'd be able to keep his distance. For one thing there wouldn't be any need to breathe with her every damn night. And there would be no more baby to feel kick. The need for back rubs would subside. The intimacy of their situation had been just that—situational—and Jed expected it would change.

It did. It got worse.

He didn't breathe with her anymore; now he watched her nurse the baby. Instead of watching her chest rise and fall under whatever maternity top she was wearing, now he got treated to glimpses of one creamy white breast and then the other as Neile drank her fill.

He didn't have to feel Neile kick inside Brenna anymore, either. Now he ended up holding her. And the squirming baby, nestled so snugly against his shoulder, her soft brown hair tickling his neck, smelled not just of baby powder but of the same soft cinnamon-and-spice scent that he associated with Brenna.

He was going quietly out of his mind.

He grunted now, since he wasn't telling Tuck any of that.

"Well, I think it's goin' good," Tuck said when it was apparent that was all the answer he was going to get. "An' so does Gran'pa."

"Great," Jed muttered into the depths of the engine.

"An' Neile, too," Tuck went on. "She'd say so if she could talk. It's okay havin' a sister," he went on, going up on his toes and craning his neck to peer into the engine, too. His voice echoed as he talked into the compartment. "I wouldn't mind a brother next time, though."

Jed's head came up so fast he damn near cracked his skull on the hood. "You're not gettin' a brother!"

Tuck pulled back, startled. "Well, technically he'd be a cousin," he said, missing the point entirely. "But that's okay.

It's close enough for gover'ment work. That's what Gran'pa says."

"You and *Grandpa* discussed it?" Jed rubbed his head furiously.

"Yep. He'd like a boy next time, too. So, whaddya say?"

Jed strangled on his answer to that. He bent over the engine again. "Hand me the wrench," he said through his teeth.

Tuck handed him the wrench. Once more his head lined up alongside Jed's. "Whatcha gonna do with it?"

"Damned if I know."

Tuck grinned. "You like it, too, don't you?"

"Like what?"

"Bein' married. Havin' Neile. Havin' Gran'pa. An' Brenna."

He didn't *have* Brenna, Jed thought grimly, his fingers tightening on the wrench. "Don't you have some homework to do?" he asked finally, desperately.

"Nope."

"Chores?"

"Did 'em."

"How about a drawing? Aren't you drawing these days?"

"Sure. Pen and ink. Brenna's showin' me. But she's feedin' Neile right now so I thought I'd come talk to you." He bounced on one foot, then the other. "You want to see what I'm working on? It's in the studio."

"Later," Jed said. He didn't trespass into Brenna's studio. It was too personal, too much a part of her. He jerked something—he didn't know what—with the wrench. It broke off and clattered to the floor of the garage. He swore.

Tuck started for the house. "You're sure a grouch these days," he said over his shoulder. "Gran'pa says love can do that to people."

Hope and painting could only get you so far.

At least Brenna found that to be true as the days passed and Jed seemed further away than ever. She tried to tell herself that she could wait, that Neile was three weeks old. Then Neile was four weeks old.

Five weeks. Five and a half.

Six.

At last.

Brenna came downstairs earlier than usual the morning Neile turned six weeks old. She came down as soon, in fact, as she heard Jed moving around the kitchen. Ordinarily he got his own breakfast and headed out while she was still dealing with the baby. She had told him when they first married that she would see to getting Tuck off to the bus. Sometimes recently she'd regretted that, since it meant that Jed had no reason to hang around.

But this morning he was sitting at the table, his back to her, as he nursed a cup of coffee and stared out into the winter morning darkness. She stopped for just a minute to look at him. It was almost the first chance she'd had in a couple of weeks. Mostly she seemed to catch glimpses of him moving away.

He hadn't put on his hat yet, and she could see that his normally short dark hair was getting a little shaggy. The ridge from his hat band hadn't disappeared completely even overnight, and she had to squelch the urge to smooth her hand over his hair. Her fingers tightened into fists at her sides.

Not now. Not yet.

Soon.

She took a breath. "Good morning."

He jerked, slopping coffee on the table. "Oh, er, mornin'. Somethin' wrong?" He shoved his chair back and stood up.

Brenna padded into the room on slippered feet and helped herself to a cup of coffee, then leaned against the counter. "Not a thing. Just thought I'd get an early start on the day." She smiled. "Maybe make Neile a birthday cake."

"Birthday cake?" He was mopping up his coffee, not looking at her.

"She's six weeks old today." She waited expectantly.

Jed kept right on mopping coffee. Then he crossed to the sink and wrung out the rag. "That's pretty old, all right." And apparently not very significant.

On to step two. "I also wanted to catch you before you left."

He looked over at her, his expression wary.

"I have to go to the doctor this afternoon."

He scowled. "You told me there wasn't anything wrong!"

"Nothing is wrong. It's a normal six-week checkup. Mine and Neile's. And I wondered if you'd come along."

"To Neile's appointment?" He'd gone when she was a month old, so he didn't look too amazed.

"And to mine."

His eyes widened. He hesitated, then dipped his head briefly. "Yeah, okay. If you want."

So he wasn't exactly enthusiastic; still she forced a smile. "We could eat lunch in town first. The appointment's at one-thirty."

He shook his head. "Can't. I gotta help Mace out this morning. We'll prob'ly just get somethin' there. But I'll be back and pick you up at twelve forty-five." He was already grabbing his hat and starting for the door as he spoke. "See you." The door banged shut after him.

"See you," Brenna said, her voice soft with disappointment. Still she hoped. Maybe he just needed it spelled out for him.

She painted all morning while the baby slept. She fixed a noon meal for herself and her father, then bundled the baby up and got ready to go. At twelve-forty the truck came bumping down the road.

Jed leaned out the window. "Ready to go?"

The baby was, according to the doctor, "healthy as a rock."

"A rock?" Brenna echoed.

Dr. Mathis nodded. "Twelve pounds, four ounces. Nursing well. Sleeping well. What more do you want?"

"Nothing." Not from the baby, anyway.

"Now let's take a look at you," he said, patting the examining table.

"I'll take Neile," Jed said hastily, practically grabbing the baby out of Brenna's arms. "We'll wait out there." He jerked his head toward the waiting room.

"Things all right?" Dr. Mathis asked her when Jed had left.

Brenna smiled. "You tell me."

"Ah." He nodded. "Like that, is it? Well, let's see."

Brenna didn't know if she imagined the sound of his boots pacing up and down the whole time the doctor examined her, but she definitely heard the sudden reluctance with which they moved when the nurse called him back in.

"Is she dressed?" Jed came in, the baby held in front of him like a shield, as he looked from Brenna to the doctor worriedly.

"She's fine," Dr. Mathis said. "All systems go."

Jed smiled, relief clear on his face. "Thank God."

Dr. Mathis grinned. "At six weeks all fathers say that. Go ahead. Enjoy. Just be gentle."

Jed looked at Brenna, confused.

She smiled. "He means it's all right now. It's safe."

He blinked. "Huh? Safe?"

The doctor laughed and clapped him on the back. "Don't tell me you haven't been counting the days. Time's up. You can start making love again."

Brenna waited. She put on a lovely, warm, deep blue, brushed flannel nightgown and went to bed shortly after she got Neile down. And she waited.

Jed never came.

He was gone the next morning when she got up. The note on the table said, "Helping Mace."

He didn't get home until after eight that night.

"I'm bushed," he said, passing through the kitchen and barely even looking at her. "Gonna hit the hay."

The next morning was just like the last. He helped Mace and then Taggart and Noah for the rest of the week. As soon as he had their own cattle fed, he left. Taggart's barn needed a new loft. Mace's cabin needed a new room. Noah's fireplace needed cleaning. Next thing you knew, Brenna thought, God would need help with the snowfall.

No matter. Whatever the reason, Jed rarely got back until Tuck and Otis had already turned in and Brenna was nursing the baby.

He never even glanced in her room as he was passing at night. And unless she could think of something to ask him or tell him, he didn't stop. He scarcely looked her way.

He acted as if he wanted nothing at all to do with her.

But Brenna began to think the opposite might very well be true.

She'd seen him act this way once before—eleven years ago—when he'd been afraid to ask her for a date.

"Didn't reckon you'd have time for a good-for-nothin' cowboy like me," he'd told her after. After—

After she'd made the first move for him.

She'd watched him out of the corner of her eye for weeks, waiting for him to take the initiative, waiting for him to get up the guts to ask her out, to at least come and sit on the porch in the evening and talk to her. She could see his interest in his face.

But he didn't make a move. She did finally, when there had been a band down in Livingston she'd wanted to hear. Mustering her courage, she'd asked Jed to take her.

"Daddy will let me have the truck if I have someone with me coming back late at night," she'd told him. It was the truth.

He'd looked so astonished that she remembered blushing, afraid she'd been wrong about all those desperate looks. "It was just a thought. You don't have to."

"I want to!" He blurted the words, then colored even more furiously than she had. "I'd like that," he'd said more quietly.

And that was how it had begun.

He hadn't kissed her, either, until she'd kissed him. Then he'd kissed like there was no tomorrow. But even though he'd been eager, even desperate to make love to her, he'd stopped when she'd wanted to.

"I understand," he'd said raggedly. "We'll wait."

They'd been waiting now for eleven years.

Did he, perhaps, still think she wanted to wait?

Good grief, he couldn't, Brenna thought. But maybe, being Jed, he did. Maybe, being Jed, and their marriage having come about the way it did, he was waiting for the okay from her.

Fine, she would make the first move.

* * *

You can start making love again.

Jed heard those words in his sleep. They haunted his dreams and, unfortunately, all his waking hours, too.

You can start making love again. It's safe now.

There's a laugh, he thought. Safe? Ha.

And now that he'd been given the go-ahead, nothing else in their marriage was safe, either. He couldn't just enjoy spending time with her now. Expectations had changed.

Expectations he couldn't fulfill.

So he'd disappeared the moment they'd arrived home from the doctor's that afternoon; he'd been disappearing regularly every day since.

He tried to slip into the house to spend a little time with Tuck and Otis when she was busy with the baby. He attempted to spend a few minutes with the baby when Brenna was busy painting. he did his very best never to be alone with her.

It worked, too, for all of ten days.

On the eleventh he came home even later than usual, dirty and tired. He'd worked with Taggart on the ranch all day and had helped Mace in the cabin all evening. It was ten-thirty by the time he drove into the yard. Upstairs all the lights were out when he let himself in.

Only the lamp by the couch in the living room was still lit, but the room was empty. Brenna had put the sheet and blankets on it for him, then gone to bed. Jed looked longingly at the couch, tempted to fall on it without bothering to take a shower. Only a glimpse of his dirty jeans and grimy face in the mirror on the closet door convinced him he'd better.

He hung up his jacket and tiptoed up the steps, easing his way past Brenna's darkened room, breathing easily only when he shut the bathroom door. He stripped off his filthy clothes, then stepped into the shower. Hot water cascaded over him. He sighed and flexed his shoulders, trying to ease the tightness there and the soreness in his back.

He could have used a back rub. He wondered if Brenna would be willing to give him one. He wasn't so tired that his body didn't respond to the idea.

He groaned and flicked the tap, shutting off the hot completely and ducking his head under the icy stream that was left.

Take that, he told himself. *It's all you're going to get.*

He was still shivering even after he'd dried off. He rubbed his wet hair until it was damp and spiky, then pulled on a clean pair of shorts and jeans, zipping them, but leaving the button undone. Just enough to be decent in case she awoke and happened to look out her bedroom door.

Then, looping the towel around his neck he gathered up his dirty clothes and opened the door.

All was quiet.

Careful to keep it that way, he padded down the hall. The door to Otis's room was slightly ajar. Soft sounds of muffled snoring came from within. Farther down the hall even softer sounds came from Tuck's room.

Jed didn't hesitate outside Brenna's room to listen to the sound of her breathing, to see if he could hear the faint murmur of Neile in the alcove. In fact, he dropped his clothes in the hamper and hurried past, down the stairs again.

In the pool of light from the table lamp he saw her waiting, curled up on the couch.

He stopped dead. "What are you doing?"

She smiled faintly. "I wonder if you'd mind rubbing my back."

He stared at her. "Rub. Your. Back."

She nodded, looking up at him. Her tousled hair was a coppery halo in the golden lamplight. "If you wouldn't mind." She sounded very matter-of-fact.

He swallowed. His hands went up to grip the ends of the towel he'd slung around his neck. He needed something to hang on to. "But . . . you're not pregnant anymore."

"No, I'm not."

"Then—"

"We don't need that as an excuse."

He opened his mouth but no sound came out.

"And I do have a backache," she went on. "Neile's no lightweight." Her tone was even again. "Sometimes carrying her around hurts my back. So . . . would you?"

Jed shifted from one booted foot to the other. His hands twisted in the towel. He scraped it back and forth across his bare shoulders, praying for deliverance. It didn't come.

Brenna waited, her eyes never leaving his. "Jed?"

He sighed and gave a jerky nod. "If you want." He shut his eyes briefly, then opened them and started back up the steps. "Come on."

"Where?" She sounded confused.

"To your room. Where else?"

"Neile's been restless tonight. I shut off the light early so I wouldn't disturb her. So I thought we could do it here."

There? On his couch? Where he had enough trouble getting to sleep every night without the memory of her having lain there minutes before? "But—"

But Brenna was already slipping off her robe and turning onto her side. She smiled back up at him over her shoulder.

Jed felt a shudder run through him. His jaw clenched. He sent another fervent prayer winging heavenward—this one for self-control. Then he came the rest of the way down the stairs. "Lie down," he said hoarsely.

"You sound like I'm a dog." Brenna laughed.

But Jed was beyond humor. Beyond help. He stood at the edge of the couch, feet spread, hands loosely curled at his sides, like a gunfighter, waiting.

Brenna started to lie down, then sat up again. "I'll just take this off first."

And while he stood there with his mouth hanging open, she stripped her nightgown over her head and tossed it aside!

The creamy expanse of her back, the bare length of her legs lay open to his sight. Only one tiny bit of her was covered by the barest scrap of peach-colored lace. Jed sucked air.

She looked over her shoulder at him. "Jed?" The matter-of-factness was gone. There was gentle encouragement in her voice now.

Jed's lips pressed into a thin line. He gave a jerky nod, then knelt beside the couch and laid his hands on her back. A soft shiver ran through her. One ran through him. He bit his lip and began to knead.

"I'm not a loaf of bread, you know," she protested.

Abruptly he pulled his hands away. She caught one of them.

"Gentler," she admonished him softly. "Please, Jed?" *Please, Jed.* It sounded so simple. She settled down once more and closed her eyes.

Please, Jed. Suffer, he told himself. You deserve it.

He ran his thumbs ran along the ridges of her spine, played his fingers over the muscles on either side.

Brenna let out a sigh. "Yessssss."

Jed's fingers tightened reflexively. He willed them to relax, willed them to keep moving. They softened and steadied, stroked.

"'S wonderful," Brenna murmured and wriggled just a little under his touch, moving into the stroke, meeting it. Then her back arched and she gave a tiny moan.

"What's the matter?" Even to his own ears, Jed's voice was harsh.

She shook her head. "Nothing. Not a thing. It's bliss." She sighed again. "Pure bliss. Don't stop. Don't ever stop." She wriggled again.

He stopped then. Had to. If he didn't, he knew he wouldn't. Ever.

Her eyes flicked open. "Jed?"

A muscle in his jaw ticked, and he felt a hectic flush beneath the taut skin covering his cheekbones. He ran his tongue over his lips.

Brenna's were parted slightly. She looked—aroused.

Even as he thought it, she raised herself a bit and rolled onto her back, catching his hands in hers, holding them against her bare breasts. "Jed?" Her voice was soft, then. A whisper. Not a question. A promise.

He jerked his gaze away and tried to pull his hands out of hers. She hung on.

"What's wrong, Jed? Tell me." Her voice was soft. Seductive.

And Jed was within an inch of being seduced. He remembered the feeling all too well. He stiffened. Resisted. His breath came quick and shallow. "Don't!"

"I'm your wife. It's allowed." Her words were gently teasing. Her smile was tempting. "You're my husband. You're allowed, too." She let go of one of his hands to run her fingers down his bare chest.

He shuddered under her touch. His loins tightened. His fists clenched. Still not meeting her eyes, he shook his head. "No, Brenna. Don't. Stop."

She stopped, but she didn't let go of his hands. She waited.

Jed bent his head, shut his eyes and tried to blot out the need, the desire, the feelings that were consuming him. He tried to think, to speak.

"It isn't—" he tried at last. "We didn't—!" The words wouldn't come.

"It isn't part of the bargain? Is that what you're saying?" Her voice was soft, but there was no mistaking the hint of challenge in the words. "We didn't agree to make love?"

He supposed he ought to be glad she believed in plain speaking. It saved him saying them.

"No, it isn't," he said. "And we didn't." He turned back to meet her eyes fiercely, daring her to dispute it.

She didn't. But she didn't flinch away, either. She held him fast. "Fair enough. And is there a rule that says we can't amend the bargain? Add to it?"

His jaw clenched. He felt as if they were being dragged to a precipice and there was no way back. "No. There's no rule." He got the words out through barely parted lips.

She looked at him, her heart in her eyes. "Then why don't we?"

Their gazes locked. They were at the edge. Jed pulled his hands out of her grasp and pushed himself to his feet. He folded his arms across his chest. "Because I don't want to."

He watched as the warmth turned to shock in her eyes. The light died. The joy turned to ashes.

Way to go, he congratulated himself. But what the hell else could he do? "I don't want you," he lied. Then he looked away.

Slowly, almost as if she was in pain, Brenna sat up. Averting her eyes, she reached for her nightgown and pulled it back over her head. Once more the beauty of her flushed body was hidden from his gaze. Her cheeks were flushed, still, but her eyes were dark and her mouth was pale. She stood up and wrapped her robe around her, a fumbling with the sash the only evidence of her agitation. She started for the stairs, then stopped at the bottom to look back at him.

"Thank you for spelling it out for me," she said tonelessly. "I'm sorry to have bothered you. I won't do it again."

He should never have married her.

He *knew* it wouldn't work.

What kind of idiot was he to think that they could make a platonic marriage, that he could have her in his life just like he'd always wanted? Well, almost like he'd always wanted.

He couldn't.

But he couldn't give her a divorce, either. Because of Tuck.

Madger would have Tuck away from him in an instant if he did something as stupid as that.

Maybe he could let Brenna adopt Tuck. If she met somebody else—somebody she wanted to marry—the two of them could adopt Tuck, and he could just sort of disappear into the back of the beyond.

Live by himself. Be a hermit. Buy a hair shirt.

Fortunately even he wasn't quite so far gone as to believe in the sense of that . . . yet. He was far enough gone, however, to know that the platonic marriage he'd bargained on wasn't going to work.

He couldn't have half a loaf. Not when Brenna wanted it all.

He folded up the blankets and set them at the end of the sofa. He pulled on a shirt, grabbed his jacket, stuffed his feet in his boots. Then he wrote her note and left it on the kitchen table. It didn't say much—just: "I'll be staying at the cabin if you need me."

There was nothing else left to say.

"If I need you?" Brenna read the letter aloud to herself in the light of early morning. Her throat ached with the tears she'd shed in the night. Her heart ached with the hopes Jed had trampled.

She'd made her move. She'd played her final card—and she'd lost.

"Don't worry. I won't need you, Jed," she said, her words echoing in the emptiness of the room.

If it took her the rest of her life, she'd learn never to need him again.

Eleven

Life went on.

He did the same things he'd always done. He wasn't going to shirk his duty just because he wasn't living with Brenna anymore. He fed and doctored the cattle, culling out the ones he should've got rid of earlier. He chopped ice to open water holes, cut and hauled down firewood, rode the fence line where the snow permitted, to make sure the cattle weren't drifting off the winter range.

He stopped by and talked to Tuck one day after school, explaining that he was wintering in the cabin because it gave him better access to the herd. Though it was on Taggart's land, it was, in fact, closer to the range, and Tuck might have bought it. At least he didn't argue.

He did say, "Reckon you'll get lonely."

"I'll live," Jed replied.

And he did. But he didn't wear a real penitential hair shirt, just an emotional one, because every day, everywhere he went, he carried the memories of those weeks of his life with Brenna on his back and in his heart.

He missed her.

He'd missed her eleven years ago, after he'd walked away from her that time. But he'd felt noble then. Righteous. Determined.

Now all he felt was miserable.

He was being noble, he assured himself. He was doing the right thing. And eventually he would be glad. He would be justified.

But right now all he did was hurt.

She hoped he was as miserable as she was.

She hoped he missed the colicky baby and the dirty diapers and the long division and the grumpy old man. She hoped he missed her.

She missed him. More than she wanted to. More than she thought possible. More than the first time.

It wasn't fair that he should do this to her twice! She fumed with anger, trying to paint away her frustration. And then she remembered what she had told Neil. *Life isn't fair.*

"You didn't have to demonstrate," she railed aloud at God. "I already knew that. Did You think I'd forgotten?"

Apparently He didn't think a reminder was amiss.

Still, she wasn't sorry she'd married Jed. Wasn't sorry that she'd dared to hope. Dared to risk.

It would have been more foolish to say no to a man she'd loved for longer than she could remember. It would have been folly not to try to make it work. Regrets came when you *didn't* do things, not when you did.

Eventually she'd believe that. Eventually.

But right now as she painted her cowboy, she could barely see him for the tears.

He'd told Tuck to tell him when things needed doing at the ranch house. He didn't want to neglect things just because he wasn't there. But days went by, a week, then two, then three and more. He saw Tuck in the barn and in the field, and twice the boy had come to the cabin to bring him mail. But he had no call to go to the house.

Then one afternoon when he rode up to the cabin, he saw a light on already. And when he went in, Tuck was there.

He said, "I came to tell you that you can help pack."

The word hit Jed in the gut. "Pack?" he echoed. *She was leaving?* "To go...where?"

"New York. Brenna's got a show."

"Oh. A show." He almost sagged with relief. "Pack paintings, you mean?"

"For now," Tuck said.

Which meant...what?

Jed frowned. "What do you mean, for now? Is she thinking about moving back to the city?"

"She an' Gran'pa talk about it." The boy didn't seem overly concerned. He zipped up his jacket and started toward the door. "I guess it'd be okay. Don't know how I'll like New York, though."

Jed stared. She was planning on taking Tuck?

Yeah, probably she was. She had taken over since he seemed to have abdicated his responsibility.

Would she have bothered to tell him? he thought, indignation rising. But then it dropped again, because for all that he'd been around, why should she even think he cared?

"We're goin' to the show," Tuck said. "All of us. Even Gran'pa." His eyes were alight now. He looked eager, happy.

"When?"

"Thursday."

In just two days. "When does she want me to help with the packing?"

"She doesn't. She told me to ask Taggart." He opened the door, then turned to look back at his uncle. "I thought you'd rather I asked you."

Yes. He would. He did.

They were married. It was his responsibility to help. And say goodbye. And wish her well.

By the following afternoon he'd finally mustered up the guts to do it.

She wasn't there.

"Went into Livingston," Otis told him. "She'll be sorry she missed you."

Jed wondered if he imagined the scorn in the old man's voice. He started to open his mouth to reply. He closed it again. There was nothing he could say.

He looked around the living room. Tuck and Brenna had a jigsaw puzzle half-finished on the table. A new baby-rocking swing sat near the window with a clear view of the bird feeder. Was Neile big enough to notice birds now? Otis was walking better. Steadier on his feet. Less shuffling.

They were doing just fine without him.

"Pictures're in the studio," Otis grunted, turning his back and heading for the kitchen. "Go to it."

Jed went. He'd seen Brenna pack some of her smaller watercolors and sketches before. He'd lent a hand once or twice, back before Neile was born. He knew what to do, and he was glad to do it. And he had to admit to more than a little curiosity about what she'd been painting. More hardworking, hard-driving cowboys? Or was she past that now?

He let himself into the studio at the back of the house. It had always been *her* place, and he hadn't intruded except when she'd invited him. Now he stood in its silence and felt, even in the emptiness, her presence everywhere.

Her visions—in a hundred quick sketches—wrapped around him.

The mountains and valleys they both loved. The cattle. The horses. And more.

Their friends and family. Tuck. Neile. Otis. Taggart. Felicity. Noah. Tess. Mace and Jenny. All the children. Everyone was clearly identifiable. Not faceless generic cowboys, but real people. Laughing. Working. Playing. Touching.

But none of him.

He didn't think he could hurt any more than he already did. But seeing everyone that mattered in her drawings—without him—caused an ache so raw he had to turn away.

He looked around for the larger paintings that he was supposed to pack, needing to do something, to stop thinking. He spied a sack leaning against the far wall and hurried over. He told himself it wouldn't matter if they were larger versions of the people he'd just turned away from. He could pack them. He *would* pack them. And then he'd get out of here. Go on his way.

He jerked the sheet off the first painting, then stopped—and stared.

Tuck was in the painting—grinning as he threw a loop over a fence post. But he wasn't alone in his joy at the accomplishment. With him, beaming like a proud parent, was Brenna's ubiquitous cowboy. Same blue chambray shirt. Same faded, dusty Wranglers. Same battered nondescript hat.

Only, the cowboy's hat didn't hide his face in this painting. His head wasn't turned or shadowed or obscured to make him Every Cowboy.

He was real. He was specific. He was Jed.

No. He couldn't be!

She'd just used the same general clothing on the earlier cowboy. He simply resembled her cowboy hero. He strode over to study two earlier ones she had hung on the far wall.

When he'd seen them before, he'd paid attention to the sense of movement, the mood and tone. Now he looked more closely at the man, searching, doubting.

Finding.

Small things. Tiny penciled details in the stitching on the boots the cowboy wore. They were barely noticeable. All the attention was on the skill of the cowboy cutting the steer out of the herd. But Jed knew those boots; he was wearing them.

In the other he found half-shadowed words on a belt buckle that confirmed it. WOLF POI...BULL-RID...CHAM... was all that was visible. But Jed knew what they said. He had only to glance down at his own worn buckle to read: WOLF POINT BULL-RIDING CHAMPION.

He moved back to the new paintings, yanking the drape off the next one.

And found the same thing.

The same cowboy. This time playing cribbage with Otis. The old man's hand was trembling over the cribbage board. The young man's fists were curled tight on the tabletop so he wouldn't reach out and help Otis stuff the damn matchstick in. Jed recalled the feeling all too well. He let out a shaky breath.

This was a hero?

He found his own hand trembling as he uncovered the next painting. In it he found himself face-to-face with his own image seated in the rocking chair by the Christmas tree, an expression of pure bliss on his face as he looked down at the baby asleep in his arms.

In each of those there was a woman in the background, watching, smiling. A shadowy benevolent presence. A hint of Brenna?

He couldn't help smiling. He looked at it for a long while, then went on.

In the fourth painting the woman was gone.

The cowboy was there—*Jed* was there—but now he stood alone.

No Tuck. No Otis. No Neile. Even the shadowy woman was gone. He was alone. Bare-chested and hatless, clad only in jeans. His hair was spiky, as if it had just been washed, and there was a towel around his neck. He was clutching that towel so tightly his knuckles were white with the strain.

Jed remembered the feeling very well. But if he hadn't, the expression on his face in the painting was such a mixture of anguish and despair, it would have come back full force. Just seeing it made his insides clench again now. He turned away.

There was one more painting left. Carefully Jed lifted the drape.

It was Jed, again, in all his cowboy trappings, striding straight toward the viewer. He looked strong, stoic, resolute, determined. His jaw was tight, his shoulders taut. Brave. The mythic cowboy hero.

Behind him, clinging to the porch railing, watching him go, was Brenna.

No longer smiling. No longer shadowy. No. Now she was all too clear. She looked shattered, unprotected. The anguish of love—and loss—was vivid on her face.

It was an expression Jed had never seen before—because, he realized, it was the first time he'd ever looked outward, not inward, when he was leaving.

"Oh, God," he muttered.

He looked at Brenna again. Then at himself walking away from her. Strong. Resolute. Determined.

Brave?

Heroic?

Hell, no. He was a coward.

He shut his eyes. It didn't help. He saw clearly for the first time what he had done.

There was champagne, and there were canapés. There were more people in black than she'd seen at any funeral—always a good sign, according to Loren. "Money, don't you know?" And—also a blessing according to Loren—only two people with nose rings and one man with purple hair. There was a woman with a camera and another shooting video, and a man Loren had identified as "press." There were Sold signs on seventeen of her thirty paintings. Loren was walking on air.

"Mill," he said in Brenna's ear. "Schmooze. Be the artistic *wunderkind* we all know you are."

Brenna growled at him over her champagne glass filled with soda. She waved it in front of her, using it like a sword to keep people at bay. "When can I go home?" she murmured.

"Later."

"But—"

"Enjoy, dearest. This is what you work for!"

It wasn't. Not at all. But she didn't think she'd ever get Loren to understand that. He was wonderful at what he did, which was bringing people and paintings together. That was more than enough. She didn't need him to understand the rat's nest of emotions that went on inside her head when she put her pencil and brushes to paper. She didn't need him to know she'd rather be two thousand miles away right now.

"Your father is delighted," Loren said. "You see how he smiles."

He smiled like that when his feet hurt and his collar was too tight, Brenna thought. But bless him, Otis had put on a suit for her, and now he was nodding his head just like he really believed what some Upper East Side socialite was saying.

"The boy, too." Loren nodded at Tuck, who was standing on first one foot and then the other next to the refreshment table. He had a silly grin on his face, and Brenna devoutly hoped it wasn't from the champagne. She hoped it was because they were showing ten of his sketches, too.

"It was a brilliant idea," Loren said now, "putting up his work."

That had been Brenna's suggestion. She'd brought along several of Tuck's sketches to show Loren, both because she wanted his assessment of the boy's talent, and because she thought having his view of the ranch tradition counterpoint her own would be good for both of them.

Loren had agreed at once.

When they told Tuck, he'd goggled at them. "You're showin' my work, too? Here?" He'd beamed at Loren's nod. Then slowly his grin had faded. "Jed isn't here."

Jed wasn't there.

Wherever she was, Jed wouldn't be, Brenna knew, though she couldn't tell Tuck that.

"You can save him a program," she'd said. He could take his uncle photos and even a video. She hoped that would be enough.

She studied the boy now, willing him to look at her. To smile. But he was looking past her toward the door. Probably, like her father, he was wishing he could make a bolt for it. Lucky Neile, who got to be baby-sat by one of Brenna's friends.

All at once Tuck broke out in a grin, shoved himself away from the wall and darted toward her. Brenna started to smile. But he didn't even notice. He sailed right past her.

"Jed!" he shouted. "You came."

Jed had never been so glad to see anyone in his life. He grabbed the boy and hauled him into his arms, squeezing him so tight that Tuck said, "You're squishin' me!"

"Sorry." He eased his grip a tad and lowered Tuck back to the ground, but still hung on. Over Tuck's shoulder he saw Brenna. She looked dazed.

"Didja see?" Tuck demanded. "Didja see my stuff?"

Jed, looking at Brenna, barely heard him. "Stuff? What stuff?"

Tuck's arm swept toward one wall. "Look!" And there they were—the sketches of the bull-riding, others of a branding. Tuck's work—right up there alongside Brenna's.

"Well, I'll be—" A slow smile spread across Jed's face. "How'd that happen?"

"Brenna did it. Didn't she tell you?"

Jed shook his head. He was walking now, steering the boy, moving across the room, parting the sea of penguin-and-mutant art lovers, heading toward Brenna. "She didn't tell me."

"Then why'd you come?" Tuck asked and Jed saw the same question in Brenna's eyes.

He kept moving until he could stop square in front of her. Their eyes met. This time Jed didn't look away. "I came because I love you," he said.

"I knew it!" Loren was chirping as he practically pirouetted around the now empty gallery, gloating over all the Sold signs and the fact that Brenna's husband had come to see her succeed.

"I knew he'd be here. I knew it! All this garbage about not being able to leave the cows, darling! How could you think I'd believe it? Cows have gotten by for thousands of years with no one to hold their hooves." He giggled at his own humor.

Brenna ignored him. She expected to wake up at any moment and discover that someone had stolen her flute of club soda and replaced it with the world's most potent champagne. She wondered, in fact, if she didn't hope that was the case. If it was, then she was just imagining the cowboy at her side.

Had he really said, "I love you"?

He certainly hadn't said anything else. But even though he never spoke, he'd stayed at her side for the rest of the night.

He wasn't budging now, either, just standing there, quiet, steady, while Loren chuntered on. At last Loren ground to a halt and took both Brenna's hands in his.

"You should be thrilled." It was a command, not a comment.

"Oh, I am," Brenna said faintly. She had no idea if it was true or not. She wouldn't until she understood what Jed was doing here.

Loren turned and pumped Jed's hand. "She is a wonder," he said. "Such perception. Such sensitivity. Such a grasp of life."

"Loren!" Brenna protested.

"It's the truth. Ask your husband. He is after all the subject of your work, darling." He giggled again. "Very sly, that. From the mythic American hero to the man in your life!" He winked at Brenna, who felt her face flame.

"Go." He pushed her into Jed's arms, then looked past her into his eyes. "You're a lucky man, my friend."

"I hope so," Jed said.

He bore Tuck's chatter and Otis's gimlet-eyed glances all the way back uptown. He withstood Brenna's silence. He waited, held his peace, focused on the job ahead. The only thing that even momentarily distracted him was when they went into the apartment Brenna and Neil had shared and he saw Neile for the first time in weeks.

"My God, she's grown!" He reached for her. The baby's head bobbed only briefly and barely needed the support of his hand. Her eyes wavered, jerked, then focused on him. He stared, astonished at how much she'd changed.

And then she smiled.

Jed's heart caught in his throat. He smiled back for just a moment. Then wordlessly he handed her back to the woman—one of Brenna's friends, he supposed—who had been holding the baby. He nodded politely to her, then turned to Brenna.

"Will you come with me?"

"Come with you? Where?"

He gave her the name of the hotel the travel agent in Bozeman had booked for him. He'd never been to New York, had had no idea where to go. It was satisfactory, even though it cost the earth.

Tonight—he knew—that was the smallest price he was going to pay.

She hesitated. "Will you be all right?" she asked her father.

He nodded. "We will." He shot a worried look at Jed, then a searching look at his daughter. "Will you?"

She turned her gaze on Jed. "You love me?"

Gravely he nodded.

She looked back to her father. "I'll be all right," she said.

"I didn't want to leave you."

They were in his hotel room now, and he stood with his back to her, staring out the window. He didn't know how to begin. He had no finesse. Nothing but the truth—which, God knew, he owed her.

"Not last month. Not eleven years ago." He bent his head and gazed down forty stories at the lights and cars and people and didn't see any of them. His forehead rested against the glass. "I told myself I was being noble, walking out."

"What!" Brenna practically bounced off the bed where she'd been sitting.

He turned and faced her. His mouth twisted. "Noble. Brave. Sacrificing what I wanted for the greater good. *Your* good."

"Mine? I don't understand."

"I know. I didn't want you to." He gave a heavy sigh. "I still don't."

A frown creased her brow. "Why?"

Jed shoved a hand through his hair. "Because it wasn't nobility at all. It was cowardice. And pride."

She looked at him. He wanted—desperately—to look away. He wanted to turn—and run.

Funny how riding off into the sunset could look heroic from one angle and cowardly as hell from another. He closed his eyes and gave a small shake of his head.

He felt rather than saw her approach him. Her fingers touched his wrist, slid down and wrapped around his hand. "Tell me." Her voice was no more than a whisper. She drew him down beside her on the bed.

Tell her. He hunched his shoulders, stared at his feet. "You remember the night? The shipping?"

"I remember." Her fingers squeezed his.

"You remember after...when we walked down by the barn?"

They'd been touching all night. Small brushes. Little strokes. The aching tentative touches of young unsated love. The party had broken up. It was late, and finally he'd had to go back to the bunkhouse. Brenna had walked out with him—to hold his hand, to walk hip to hip, to stop and linger and kiss.

"I remember."

They'd parted only reluctantly, because they loved each other, because they'd agreed to wait, because it was important to do things right.

Jed sucked in his breath. "When I got back to the bunkhouse, everybody else had gone into town drinking. I was alone. Wanting you."

He knew she could hear in his voice, remember in her own mind, just how desperately.

"I was getting ready to take a shower. I'd just taken off my boots and shirt, and there was this knock on the door." He turned his head and looked at her. "I thought it was you."

God, how he'd prayed it would be Brenna, come to say that she loved him too much to wait, that she'd changed her mind, that she didn't care about doing things right, that she wanted him now!

He'd opened the door feeling equal parts anxious and desperate.

"It was Cheree."

Brenna's hand tensed around his. He slanted a glance at her, but all he could see of her bent head was the fall of her hair and the tip of her nose. He could barely hear her breathe. She didn't say a word.

"She was looking for Eddie. You remember Eddie?" A hard-riding, wild-living, two-fisted buckaroo who'd come and gone that season.

Brenna nodded. "Not . . . looking for you?" She tipped her head slightly and he could see the doubt in her eyes.

"Not me," he said firmly. Then he sighed. "But she decided to settle for me."

Brenna turned her head fully then and looked at him, her eyes searching.

He wanted to look away, to hide his guilt. His throat worked. He'd thought this would get easier. That once he started talking it would just all pour out. He should've known it would be like pulling teeth.

"She came in and sat down to wait for Eddie while I took my shower. By the time I got out, she was bored waiting for Eddie, and she thought it would be fun to play a few games with me." His voice was bitter now.

Not at Cheree. At himself.

He should have seen trouble when it came knocking. He should have realized he was no match for her, taken one look and run the other way.

But hell, he was twenty-one. A grown man.

A very frustrated, horny grown man. A man for whom a cold shower had done nothing more than to make him aware of how badly he wanted the real thing. It hadn't taken Cheree long to get things going her way.

Jed sat hunched now, his fingers laced together between his knees, staring at the floor and remembering the way Cheree had come up to him when he'd come out of the bath. He was wearing jeans, but he hadn't yet buttoned his shirt. She'd slipped her fingers inside it and her fingers had brushed lightly down his bare chest.

"Does Brenna touch you this way?" she'd asked him, her voice soft and sultry as hell. She'd smiled. "Does she even know how?"

Jed had shuddered under her touch. He'd backed up hastily, bumped into the edge of his bunk, sat down.

And Cheree had sat next to him.

"Does she kiss like this?" she'd asked him, her lips nibbling at his jaw, then sliding his shirt right off and tracing the line of his shoulders, nipping up his neck and his ear.

He'd groaned, his body fighting his heart.

"Shall I teach her what to do?" Cheree had asked, kissing him full on the lips, pushing him back so that he fell against the pillow. "How about if I teach you?"

He didn't give Brenna the details. He didn't think she'd want to hear them. He didn't want to remember them himself.

"I betrayed you." His voice was ragged. He couldn't look at her.

Not the next day. Not now. He stared down at their hands. She still held his. She heard his words—and she didn't let go.

"I thought you loved her." Her words were so quiet he barely heard them. He wasn't sure even then he heard them right.

He turned his head. "You thought I loved her?" He was amazed.

She nodded. "I knew she went down there. I heard her come back. I saw her come in, and she looked like the cat that got the cream. The next morning at breakfast, she...she told me what a man you were!"

"What a man I was?" He gaped at her.

Brenna nodded, anguished, her memories apparently every bit as tormented as his. "You wouldn't look at me after. I thought it was because you'd gone to bed with a real woman and you didn't want me anymore!"

Jed buried his face in his palm. He dragged in a desperate breath, then lifted his head and shook it. Oh God.

He turned to Brenna. She was still looking stricken.

"No," he said. "It wasn't like that." He shook his head again. "What a man I was? She said that?" The words haunted him. Something halfway between a laugh and a sob shuddered through him. "I never even made love to her."

Brenna stared at him. "But you just said—"

"I said 'betrayed you.' I did. I loved *you*. Not Cheree. But I would have had sex with her that night because she was there and I wanted it and I was aching and horny and too stupid to say no."

"But you didn't!"

"Because we didn't get that far. Because I was too quick for her." He met her eyes for just an instant, then dropped his gaze to stare between his toes. "'Premature ejaculation' they call it," he said tonelessly.

"I know what they call it," Brenna said. "So?"

His head jerked up. "So?" He looked at her, incredulous. "Didn't you hear her callin' me 'Quickdraw McCall' the next day?"

"I thought it was an affectionate nickname."

He grimaced. "So affectionate that the last thing she said to me was—" he almost couldn't get the words out, the memory was so harshly burned into his mind "—'Come and see me when you're man enough.'"

This time he couldn't look at Brenna.

He hadn't been man enough for Cheree. He hadn't dared wait around to find out if he was man enough for Brenna. Especially not after, to his way of thinking, he'd betrayed her.

So he'd left her, telling himself it was the right thing to do, the noble thing to do.

Never once, until he'd seen her view of things in her paintings, had he seen it as cowardly. Until that moment he hadn't faced the knowledge that for eleven years he'd cared more about his own pride than about the woman he professed to love.

At least he'd finally been man enough to admit that.

As for the other—well, he wasn't sure he was man enough even now. One humiliation like that had been enough for a lifetime.

"I never made love to Cheree," he said in a low voice. He was talking to his toes. "I've never made love to—or had sex with—anybody."

He felt as if all of New York City had ground to a halt. He felt as if the silence in the world went on and on. And on.

Out of the corner of his eye he could see Brenna's fingers twist together. She didn't say anything. Forever. And then, finally, she said, "Never? You're a..."

He said the word for her. Harshly. "*Virgin*. Isn't that the word for a guy who hasn't got the guts?"

She opened her mouth, but he plunged on. "When I walked away from you back then, I thought I was being noble! What I was being was proud. And scared. I didn't want you looking at me the way Cheree looked at me. I'd failed once. I was damned if I was going to fail again." He rubbed a hand over his face. "I was still proud...and still afraid last month...the night you asked me to your room."

Brenna went completely still. He couldn't imagine what she must be thinking. He didn't want to imagine, that was certain!

Her fingers unclasped, stole out and closed around his. Her voice was soft, bare inches from his ear. "And now, Jed? What now?"

"I'm tired of bein' proud. I'm sick of bein' scared." He tipped his head to the side and met her eyes. In them he saw the warmth and love and caring he'd wanted and feared so long. His mouth twisted. "I'm sure as hell done with pretendin' to be noble. I reckon I might not be much good at it, but I would . . . like to make love. With you."

In her dreams Brenna had made love with Jed since she was seventeen years old. She'd loved him in fields and in meadows, on mountaintops and along riverbanks. She'd loved him in the bunkhouse and in the bed in her father's house. She'd loved him in the tiny cabin he and Tuck had shared. In her heart she had loved him everywhere, every day.

In reality she'd always been denied.

Now, in this broad bed, in—of all places—an anonymous New York hotel room (she couldn't remember ever having dreams about that!) she gave him all the love she'd dreamed of, all the love she'd ever wanted to give him and been forced to save.

She started slowly with the buttons of his shirt. It was new. Bought for the occasion? she wondered. She ran her hands over the slick starched cotton of his shirtfront as she pulled it apart to expose his chest. She leaned forward and pressed a kiss in the center of his chest. Her lips could feel the hammer of his heart. Her own kept pace.

His hands skimmed over her shoulders, down her arms. She could feel the fine tremor in his fingers.

Oh, Jed, she thought. *I do so love you.*

She lay back on the bed and watched as he shrugged off his shirt, then came to lie beside her. When he had, she wrapped her arms around him. "This is the first time we've been in bed together."

He grimaced wryly. "Not counting all those back rubs, you mean?"

"You weren't *in* the bed. I just wished you were." She ran a finger down the line of his jaw, then touched it to his lips.

"I did, too," he said. His voice was ragged.

She smiled. "What would you have done if you had been?"

"Want me to show you?"

"Oh, yes."

He lifted her hair away from her face, then stopped. His own was serious, no sign of a smile at all. "I don't know if—" He looked worried. "What if—"

Brenna touched his lips and stopped the words. "The only *if* that matters," she told him, "is if you will love me forever the way I love you."

At her question, the blue of his eyes seemed to darken and deepen. Gravely he nodded. "I will. I do."

"Then everything else will be fine."

It would, she was certain. And if he wasn't certain, she would make him so. "I'll show you," she whispered, and she set about doing just that.

Brenna wasn't by any stretch of the imagination a skilled lover. She hadn't had the practice for that. The love she'd shared with Neil had been intense, but of necessity, gentle. It hadn't been consummated many times.

But the few times it had, she'd learned enough to know that sharing was the most important part. The physical sensations were wonderful, but secondary to the intimate connection that came from the heart.

She loved Jed. He loved her.

If she'd doubted that, she did no more. She had proof. He'd risked his pride, his heart, his soul to share himself with her.

"Kiss me," she whispered. And he did.

"Touch me," she murmured. And he did.

"Love me," she breathed.

And he did that, too.

No finesse, McCall, he told himself. No delicacy. Just hunger. And desire. And the urgent, desperate need to be a part of her.

He tried to go slow. He tried to stretch things out. "Foreplay," he'd read somewhere, "is all."

He hoped not.

If it was, he was lost before he'd even begun.

He wasn't great with buttons and zippers. It had been years since he'd fumbled with the clasp of her bra. He didn't do badly slipping her panties off. But just seeing her lying there, naked and welcoming, on the bed before him, almost caused him to lose it right there.

He shut his eyes. His chest heaved. His fists clenched. He felt like a fool. Like some teenager about to disgrace himself.

Brenna shifted, touched his knee.

He opened his eyes. She was smiling. And then she reached for him, drew him down, wrapped her legs around him, took him in.

He tensed, then shuddered, then went still. He could feel her heart beating against his. He could feel her toes pressing against the back of his thighs, her fingers in his hair, the center of her pulse around him.

Slowly, hardly daring to, he lifted his chest away from her, went up braced on his hands to look down into her eyes once more. And then, with his eyes locked on hers, never leaving them for an instant, he began to move.

It wasn't finesse. It certainly wasn't skill. And God knew he didn't think he had an inborn talent for this sort of thing, but the look on her face as he loved her told him he was doing something right. And when she twisted and turned and clutched him to her, when she shattered the same time he did, he felt like they'd conquered the world.

He dropped lightly against her, still holding himself on his hands so as not to hurt her. But she took his hands and pulled them out so he couldn't help collapsing on her. "Brenna! I'll hurt you."

"No. You did that already when you walked away." She framed his face with her hands. "Now you're staying right here. Aren't you?" There was no hesitancy in her voice when she asked, only the certainty that at last she had the answer.

"Forever," he promised and kissed her.

There were tears on her cheeks. Hers? His? He didn't know. He didn't care.

They said the words together. "I love you."

"Told you so," Tuck said.

Jed grunted. "Know-it-all."

He was bent over Otis's damned Suburban again, trying to figure out what he'd done wrong this time. He was having trouble concentrating, though. His mind, as well as his heart and soul—everything, in fact, but his body—was back in the house with Brenna. They'd been home from New York for three weeks. The best three weeks of his life.

She was painting. "The definitive cowboy portrait," she'd told him. "The essence of the man of my dreams."

"You're not paintin' me naked!" Jed had protested, knowing by now how her mind worked.

But Brenna had just giggled. "You'll see."

He reckoned he would, but he was damned if anyone else was going to! They'd be keeping that painting in the back of their bedroom closet just for them to see.

"She's a good rancher and a good painter and a good mom," Tuck went on. "The best." He was going to get an admission out of Jed if he had to hang over the fender with him all day. "Isn't she?"

Jed didn't find it hard to admit. "Yes." He turned the wrench one more time. "Get in and start it up."

Tuck got in. He turned the key. The engine sputtered, coughed and finally purred to life. Tuck beamed. Jed grinned. He swiped a greasy hand across his forehead.

Hands slipped around his waist from behind. A pair of warm lips pressed against his bare back. They felt delicious against his skin which was cool from the early spring breeze. "I'm filthy," he protested.

"You are," the lips agreed. The hands played over his ribs, teasing.

He made a sound deep in his throat. "You're askin' for trouble, lady."

"Mmm," the lips said. "Indeed." One finger played with his belt buckle.

"Brenna," he warned. "The boy's watching."

"So he is," she said. "Good. He should learn what married people do when they love each other."

"Not everything!"

"No. Some things he can learn on his own. Later. But this he needs to see." The finger traced the waistband of his jeans. There was activity below the belt that Jed knew she was quite aware of, that Tuck would never see.

"Don't start anything you aren't willing to finish," he told her.

She turned him in her arms. "I'm quite willing," she said, planting a kiss on his mouth and drawing him toward the house. "I came to tell you that I've finished the paintings. Come and see."

Tuck just grinned as Brenna towed Jed away.

He took a shower first. He insisted on it. He felt self-conscious, knowing what they were going to do right in the middle of the day, knowing that Tuck and Otis and, for all he knew, Neile and every horse and cow on the place, knew it, too!

He put on clean jeans after his shower. He buttoned up a fresh shirt and tucked it in. Maybe he'd misinterpreted. Maybe she was only going to show him the paintings. Maybe he'd be back down digging fence posts in half an hour, he thought as he padded out of the bathroom.

"Self-deception is a wonderful thing, don't you think?" Brenna said in a throaty voice. She was standing in the doorway to the bedroom, smiling.

Jed started toward the stairs. She took his hand and drew him into their room. "I thought we were going to your studio."

"Did you?" She smiled. "Think again." And she shut the door behind them.

There on the wall she'd hung two paintings. In one he was, as he'd feared, bare as the day he was born.

At least he knew he was bare. In the soft watercolors the profile of his entire length was bathed in a golden light as he lay covering her. It was as if Brenna had stood to the side, painting them as they loved.

He knew she couldn't have been. He knew that whenever they loved she was with him all the way. She loved loving him as much as he loved loving her.

And with her painting she showed him, just as she'd shown him what he was missing earlier, the love they were bringing to completion.

The other painting, surprisingly, showed it even more clearly. It was the flip side of the one she'd shown in New York, the one in which he'd seen her desolation as he'd resolutely walked away.

In this one he was coming home, strong and tall and equally determined—wearing clothes, he was relieved to note. And the joy on Brenna's face as she greeted him was marvelous to behold.

He stood looking at them, feeling tears edge his eyelids, feeling his throat tighten. "Yes," he said, and then he turned to her and took her in his arms. "Oh, yes."

They were in bed. Again.

Holding, cuddling, kissing. Loving.

"Just makin' up for lost time," Jed said, when Brenna teased him about it. "You want me to leave, just throw me out."

"Mmm." She kissed his ear.

A sweet shiver ran through him. It was always like this. Enough to set a guy to thinking he ought to see if he couldn't come up with a job that kept him closer to the house. "You wouldn't like maybe a nice fence around the flower beds you been so busy makin', would you?"

"A fence?" Brenna pulled her face away from his to look down, astonished. She knew how much cowboys liked digging postholes.

"Mmm-hmm. An' maybe another around the barn?"

"Have you got a fever, Jed?" She put a hand on his forehead. "You're not hot."

"Yes, I am." He grinned and shifted beneath her.

"What? Again?" She feigned surprise, then laughed and shifted to accommodate him.

He sighed, settled, slid home, then began gently to move in her once more. "Yeah," he mused as the feeling began to build. "Oh, yeah. An' then maybe I could build one around the garage." His back arched.

Brenna smiled and shook her head. "And then maybe one around all the fences you've already built?"

"Mmm." His head tossed. His eyes shut. "That, too."

Brenna giggled. She was moving now with him. Rocking. Making him tighten, tense. "And another around that. And another around that. And another around that. And..." There wasn't time to say any more.

"Yessssss." The world split, and all the fence posts in it came down on top of him. Brenna did, too, shuddering and laughing. And it didn't hurt a bit.

He kissed her then, and hugged her close, still smiling. He ran his fingers through her hair and savored the feel of her body snug against his. He would dig fence post holes forever to keep her at his side, but he knew he wouldn't need to.

She loved him. It still seemed a miracle, but he believed in miracles because Brenna had loved him for longer than he had known, certainly longer than he deserved. She had taken his pride and his fear and had given him, in their place, courage— and love.

"Will you come up to the cabin with me some weekend soon?" he asked. "Just me and you?" He wanted to give her a little something in return.

"To the cabin? And leave the kids with my dad?"

"Mmm. Will you?"

She raised her head, laughing. "Why? You want to put a fence in up there, too?"

He grinned wickedly. "Now there's an idea."

Brenna shook her head, still smiling. "What will Daddy say? What will Tuck say?"

Jed kissed her. "Don't ever worry about it. Otis still says, 'About time,' every morning when he sees me come downstairs. And Tuck? Well—" Jed laughed and hugged her close "—I reckon Tuck will approve."

* * * * *

More exciting, passionate CODE OF THE WEST
books are coming your way soon!
Don't miss Mace and Jenny's story,
A COWBOY'S TEARS,
coming in the Fall of 1997 from
SILHOUETTE SPECIAL EDITION!

'Tis the season for
holiday weddings!

This December, celebrate the holidays
with two sparkling new love stories—
only from

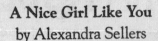

SILHOUETTE **YOURS TRULY**™

A Nice Girl Like You
by Alexandra Sellers

Sara Diamond may be a nice girl, but that doesn't mean
she wants to be Ben Harris's ideal bride. But she might
just be able to play Ms. Wrong long enough to help this
confirmed bachelor find his true wife! That is, if she
doesn't fall in love first....

A Marry-Me Christmas
by Jo Ann Algermissen

All Catherine Jordan wanted for Christmas was some
time away from the hustle and bustle. Now she was
sharing a wilderness cabin with her infuriating opposite,
Stone Scofield! But once she stood under the mistletoe
with Stone, she was hoping for a whole lot more
this holiday....

Don't miss these exciting new books,
our gift to you this holiday season!

Look us up on-line at: http://www.romance.net   XMASYT

The Calhoun Saga continues...

in November
New York Times bestselling author

NORA ROBERTS

takes us back to the Towers and introduces us to
the newest addition to the Calhoun household,
sister-in-law Megan O'Riley in

MEGAN'S MATE
(Intimate Moments #745)

And in December
look in retail stores for the special collectors'
trade-size edition of

THE
Calhoun
Women

containing all four fabulous Calhoun series books:
COURTING CATHERINE,
A MAN FOR AMANDA, FOR THE LOVE OF LILAH
and *SUZANNA'S SURRENDER.*
Available wherever books are sold.

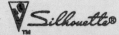

 Silhouette®

Concluding in November from Silhouette books...

This exciting new cross-line continuity series unites five of your favorite authors as they weave five connected novels about love, marriage—and Daddy's unexpected need for a baby carriage!

You fell in love with the wonderful characters in:

THE BABY NOTION by Dixie Browning (Desire 7/96)

BABY IN A BASKET by Helen R. Myers
(Romance 8/96)

MARRIED...WITH TWINS! by Jennifer Mikels
(Special Edition 9/96)

HOW TO HOOK A HUSBAND (AND A BABY)
by Carolyn Zane (Yours Truly 10/96)

And now all of your questions will finally be answered in

DISCOVERED: DADDY
by Marilyn Pappano (Intimate Moments 11/96)

Everybody is still wondering...who's the father of prim and proper Faith Harper's baby? But Faith isn't letting anyone in on her secret—not until she informs the daddy-to-be. Trouble is, *he* doesn't seem to remember her....

Don't miss the exciting conclusion of
DADDY KNOWS LAST...only in Silhouette books!

Your very favorite Silhouette miniseries
characters now have a BRAND-NEW story in

Brought to you by:

LINDA HOWARD

DEBBIE MACOMBER

LINDA TURNER

LINDA HOWARD celebrates the holidays with a **Mackenzie** wedding—once Maris regains her memory, that is....

DEBBIE MACOMBER brings **Those Manning Men** and **The Manning Sisters** home for a mistletoe marriage as a single dad finally says "I do."

LINDA TURNER brings **The Wild West** alive as Priscilla Rawlings ties the knot at the Double R Ranch.

Three BRAND-NEW holiday love stories...by romance fiction's most beloved authors.

Available in November at your favorite retail outlet.

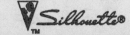